THE GIRL WITH THE
TREASURE CHEST

Dedication

For Laila

V. A. FEARON

THE GIRL WITH THE TREASURE CHEST

VILLAGE BOOKS

First published in 2013 by
Village Books

All rights © 2013 Veronica Fearon

CreateSpace paperback   ISBN: 978 1 909483 37 8

Paperback   ISBN: 978 1 909483 34 7
eBook – mobi format   ISBN: 978 1 909483 35 4
eBook – ePub format   ISBN: 978 1 909483 36 1

Produced by Kazoo Independent Publishing Services
222 Beech Park, Lucan, Co. Dublin
www.kazoopublishing.com

Kazoo Independent Publishing Services is not the publisher of this work. All rights and responsibilities pertaining to this work remain with Village Books.

Kazoo offers independent authors a full range of publishing services. For further details visit www.kazoopublishing.com

Cover design by Andrew Brown
Printed in the United Kingdom

Acknowledgements

A special thank you to Pauline Fearon, Frances Clare and Carla Leach.

Contents

Prologue		7
Chapter 1	*50/50*	12
Chapter 2	*Marie*	42
Chapter 3	*Venus*	57
Chapter 4	*Susanna*	64
Chapter 5	*The Morning After*	72
Chapter 6	*Sweets*	87
Chapter 7	*The Meet*	100
Chapter 8	*Midnight Blue*	116
Chapter 9	*Oh-ohh*	136
Chapter 10	*Looking Back*	142
Chapter 11	*Saddle Up*	154
Chapter 12	*My Suse*	161
Chapter 13	*Five, Six, Seven, Eight ...*	166
Chapter 14	*Van Job*	201
Chapter 15	*Crash*	213
Chapter 16	*No Comment*	216
Chapter 17	*In Custard*	219
Chapter 18	*Letters*	229
Chapter 19	*Trust*	241
Chapter 20	*Treasure*	251
Chapter 21	*The Skids*	258
Chapter 22	*Soldiers*	265
Epilogue		279

Prologue

"Hah!" That's the sound he makes as he crashes through the door at the foot of the stairs, stumbling as he hits the wall in front. The heels of his hands scrape against dirty brickwork.

"Why you running eh? Where you fucking going?"

He clambers to his feet before ducking as a milk bottle sails by his head and smashes against the wall. He feels the shards of glass landing in his hair and on his jacket. He can hear her shouting from the balcony above them.

"Leave him alone, Jason! Tony, run!"

He reaches back, slamming the door closed behind him to deflect other missiles.

There must be four or five of them. He hasn't looked back since he heard the shouting at the top of the stairs. His eyes dart left, then right. No time to weigh options, he hurls his body to the right.

He swaggered in last night, having eyes only for Jeanette, so now he has no clue where his car is parked. He could see it from her bedroom window, but having wound his way down so many flights of stairs with anger and threats at his tail, he can barely tell which way is up.

His footsteps reverberate against the concrete ground until he finds a stretch of grass. He rounds a corner only to come up against more concrete blocks and dead end alley-ways. Maybe the people who design and build housing estates believe that once you go in you should stay there. There's never a 'way out' sign. He can hear the traffic of the main road in front of him but the shouting behind is getting louder. He heads for the sound of cars, slaloming his way around block after block until he can run no longer. Those in the chasing pack have slowed but they're confident. They have him cornered.

He runs into a basement underneath a block, finding the room where the bins are housed. His head swims while his stomach churns at the putrid stench of rotting food and soiled nappies. He creeps to the very back, hiding behind a bin under a chute. He crouches down panting, clutching at the stitch in his side. This is why you don't go wandering onto estates you don't know.

He hears the metal clank of the door as his pursuers arrive.

"Come out little rabbit." The sing-song voice makes him shudder.

"We got something for ya."

He cowers, curling himself into a ball. The next voice is far angrier.

"You better get your fucking ass out here, now!" He knows who that is.

"Come on. We ain't gonna hurt ya. We just wanna talk."

The voices are spreading out as they move to surround him. Now he tries to hold his breath against loud metallic banging as bats, sticks and iron bars are struck repeatedly against sides of bins.

"You hear that? That's gonna be your fucking head."

They're closing in. A pair of trainers steps into sight on his right. He slides a knife from his back pocket. He has no choice. He sets his feet properly under his knees, coming up on the balls of his toes. One. Two. Three …

He springs from the corner with a loud cry, his armed right hand arcing over his shoulder. He plunges the blade into the collar-bone of the boy in front of him, using his weight to topple him to the ground. Scrambling to his feet, he tramples over the shocked, screaming youth as the others converge on him. He swipes, causing the nearest to rear back, before crashing out of the door and bolting again towards the sound of traffic.

Now they pelt across the grass after him, the chase more determined. The closest reaches out, his fingers millimetres from the billowing tail of Tony's jacket. He instinctively arches his back just in time to evade capture. There is no juice like fear as he vaults up onto the roof of a car-wreck against a high wall.

Others from the estate emerge from their flats.

"He's stabbed Owen! Get him. He's stabbed him!"

There are youths running towards him from all across the estate, as he looks frantically about. Now a barking dog is let loose.

"Seize him!"

He sees the faces of his pursuers for the first time as the angriest jumps up onto the bonnet of the car, grabbing hold of his leg, dragging him back down. He kicks, yelping with fear as the dog's panting gets louder and louder. There is a wall behind the car. It is higher but it's his only option. He drops the knife and launches himself against it, dragging himself up just as the snarling dog grabs the ankle of his jeans. He kicks out frantically with the other foot, dislodging the dog before throwing himself over the other side.

The drop is further on the other side and he lands awkwardly on his right leg. Again he cries out, scrambling to his feet as he sees the first head appear over the wall. Somehow his car is there. He hobbles across the road to it, searching his pockets desperately. At last he finds the keys, jabbing one frantically at the lock.

"You're fucking dead!"

The voices are once again advancing on him. He looks fearfully over his shoulder. One youth has landed on the other side of the wall while two others have appeared around the corner.

His hand is shaking as he tries to force the key into the lock. The bunch falls onto the drain below.

"Shit!"

He drops to his knees, unable to stop looking towards the advancing mob. He grasps at the keys, misses and instead nudges them down between the bars of the drain. The nearest assailant is only metres away.

"Fuck!"

He gets to his feet, sprinting round the car, across the road. This time someone does get a hold of his jacket as he jumps up onto the open platform at the back of the number 73 bus that has just left the stop. He clings desperately to the handrails of the stairs as two of the three youths mount the bus behind him and are trying to drag him from it. One hand loses the grip, his body twisting onto his back as they pull at his legs.

He stretches his flailing hand, seeking something to hold onto. It comes away with a baby's stroller.

"Ohhh!"

The passengers are too afraid to intervene and too shocked to move. He smashes at the head of the attacker closest to him with the stroller, kicking out and forcing him to fall into the road. The last youth hesitates just enough for Tony to stand and kick out at him. He jumps off of his own accord.

A male passenger has finally come to his senses and pulls

the bell cord repeatedly until the driver stops.

"No! No!" Tony runs the length of the lower deck banging on the driver's window. "Drive! Drive! They're gonna stab me!"

The driver looks into his rearview mirror. He turns in his seat as down in the road the injured attacker regains his feet, baring his teeth as he starts running towards the now stationary bus.

"Go!" Tony yells. "What's the matter with you? Drive! They're gonna get me!"

The driver frowns, his concern for the other passengers weighing on his mind. Then he hears the shouting of other youths running towards them from out of the estate. He turns the wheel in fright and hastily pulls out into the traffic.

The running youth jumps, reaching out just as the second gear comes to life.

The bus surges, narrowly evading him and speeds off down towards the dual carriageway.

The passengers gape, dumbfounded as Tony slumps down in the centre aisle, his back against the driver's compartment. He stretches his legs out in front of him, crossing them at the ankles and allowing a huge smile of relief to spread across his sweat-beaded face. He's still grinning when the police board the bus at the next stop.

1

50-50

Dani Fenton's midnight-blue Maserati glides across Tower Bridge, purring contentedly. She shoves her earplug in so that the hands-free wire hangs from her left ear. She thinks the other type makes her look like a tool. She presses speed dial 3 on her phone.

"Son. Where you at?" She has called him that for as long as anyone can remember. Everyone else, including his girlfriend, calls him Sonny. His real name is Ian McHale, but that seems to have been forgotten.

"Just off Hackney Road. Been round and had a look already." He's parked in a side road, smoking a zoot.

"Yeah? Who we got tonight?"

"With me? Trevor innit?"

"I weren't talking about the heavy artillery."

She's grinning. Trevor King is the type of man that if he hits you, your parents feel it. When people describe him they ignore the dirty-blond hair, the square jaw or the athletic build years of amateur boxing have given him. What they say is, he's got hands as big as plates. Those unlucky enough to meet him in precarious circumstances might also tell you he has the type of smile that forces you to check his eyes are in on it too.

Dani nods, satisfied. "I'll be there ten on the nose."

"Yep."

She pulls the wire from her ear and throws it on the passenger seat. Lowering the window she looks out east across the Thames. The sun has finally gone down and the lights from the buildings along the bank glow and gleam as they prepare to take centre stage.

Deep breaths.

She was actually asking for a roll call of who else was going to be with them tonight, but Sonny's answers are always brief. Over the years, Dani has learned to extract the maximum amount of information from the minimum amount of words he's willing to expend.

She knows now her soldiers are all in place. They're already stationed in pubs, bars or clubs in the surrounding streets. For a Meet like this, there will be between fifteen and twenty of them in groups of four or five. They're not loud or rowdy, but despite their unassuming manner, something about them still draws the eye. They all have freshly cut and groomed hair, dark shirts, black trousers and black desert boots. But it's not just about how they look. They are young, late teens, and their overly polite, softly spoken behaviour somehow gives them a slightly sinister quality.

Each group will have a button man responsible for keeping in constant contact with Sonny, who co-ordinates them all. Any break in communication with him results in a call to Mikey.

Mikey drives a truck in which he is the only occupant. The truck carries the weapons, which usually take the form of building tools that can be easily explained away. He wears overalls, steel toe capped boots and a hands free earpiece that won't leave his ear until he's back inside his home. He's parked up nearer the venue, which is a workshop under some railway arches in Bethnal Green.

Though Dani would never admit it, the truth is she is always nervous before these Meets, even the ones that aren't supposed to be that dangerous. The people she'll be in front of today are unlikely to pose any real threat to her but still there is never any room for complacency. It's 50-50 every time she sits down in the chair, no better and no worse. The people she deals with can be so unbalanced, so mistrustful that they can switch, turn, flip out in an instant. And it happens that quickly. You've always got to act as if you're on a heavy-duty job. You can't go around assuming someone's OK just because he smiled at your joke. If you don't pay attention to what you're saying and more importantly what you're hearing … You might sit there thinking you've got an idiot in front of you so you just let him waffle on, while your mind wanders to last night's bedroom activities or the football on the weekend. You're humouring him, going along with what's being said, not really understanding. The next thing you know he's getting annoyed. His voice starts to rise, heads turn. You get embarrassed so you try to laugh it off, "relax", but that only makes it worse. Too late you realise it's gonna go off. You'd go on the offensive but you really don't know what you're arguing about, which stance to take. You could be in the wrong, you just don't know. While you've been sat trying to make sense of it all, he's there, figuring out how much he's gonna hurt you and with what weapon.

If you're lucky, if you're smart, you'll jump up, grab the geezer by the throat and explain to him very clearly that you don't give a fuck what his problem is, you're not having it. No one's gonna boy (or gyal) you off and he better get hold of himself. It can go either way now, but at least you're behaving as irrationally as him. And it's back to 50-50.

Ten minutes later, she drives up to the arches. Heads turn at the distinctive sound of Dani's engine, a lioness humming her favourite tune. Sonny is already out of his car and he and Trevor are talking to members of both sides. That's deliberate. No one must feel slighted, everyone is equally important. Trevor's jollying everyone along with his "in my day we'd all jog on happily together," routine. It's not true, but he likes to emphasise the difference in age, trying to ease tension. Dani always goes on about getting everyone seated as soon as possible. Says it encourages people to kick off when they're standing because they can launch themselves at each other so easily. So she insists they always sit round a table.

She takes her time locking the hands-free wire and car stereo away and taps the accelerator with her foot, allowing the car to let out one final growl before the engine is cut. She takes a deep breath through her nostrils, clamping her mouth shut until there is a trace of a grimace.

Saddle up.

When she eventually steps out of the car, the atmosphere is ratcheted up another notch. She stands tall in black trousers and dark blue shirt. She dresses this way because she knows that it makes an impression. Besides, she's known for it now. She can't be dressing like these guys. They're young and insist on dripping with diamonds and gold, baggy jeans, big tops. Her only accessory is an expensive watch. She knows she looks good but acts as if unaware of it. She wears her hair short. Number three on top, one around the sides, curls on top accentuated by Dax. Three tramlines on the right and a white gold sleeper in her left ear complete the look.

She walks towards them, clicks the central locking device, and releases the keys into her trouser pocket. The lioness winks sagely at her admirers before closing her eyes, pulling in her ears. Her teeth remain bared.

Dani's expression is neutral as she seeks out eye contact with Trevor. He nods.

She makes sure to shake hands with Phillip, who called the Meet. He works in the youth club on the estate that Tony was chased from.

"It's nice to meet you, Dani," he says. Her eyes bore into him until he speaks again, pointing into the workshop. "It's all set up. We're ready when you are."

She glances over into the arch. Four trestle tables have been pushed together and metal chairs have been placed around them. At the farthest end, three chairs sit at the head, facing the entrance. There are ashtrays, plastic cups and bottles of water. Dani nods at Philip before turning to head inside. She can feel the gang members watching her. She doesn't want to explain why she greeted one person before another, so she keeps her eyes averted. She walks past them into the workshop and is followed by Ian who she calls "son", and Trevor who she calls "mental".

"How come you've got a white son?"

Although she is startled she doesn't show it. She'll have a wall up until she leaves. She is startled firstly by the question. Anyone who knows or has heard of her is aware they're not related, but that Sonny is always there. Some make negative comments about her supposedly favouring a white boy over her own but she never feels the need to explain. She has nothing to prove. Besides, she doesn't mean son literally. It's her way of letting him and everyone else know the value she places upon him. Simple.

But she's also startled, because the voice is female. When she turns to see who is asking stupid questions before anyone's even fucking sat down, she sees that John Bennett, one of Tony's boys, has brought his twin sister along. She doesn't answer the girl but stops walking to turn and look at Sonny. She turns back and continues to her seat. Her look says nothing but Sonny knows she is thinking – no, yelling inside her head "what sort of brain-dead fucking idiot brings his sister to a Meet?"

She's pissed off and it's putting her on edge. It's not about whether this girl can handle herself; it's about how these young, hair-trigger youths are going to behave now she's here. She's altered the group chemistry, because when Dani is in situations like this, the question of whether she's male or female is irrelevant. Like at a masquerade wearing only an eye mask as a disguise. Somehow that's enough to cloud the senses. They know Dani is a girl but they're far more interested in whether she really is what people say she is.

"This is my sister Carly," says John.

Dani glances at the sister. In those two seconds she knows she doesn't like her and that the feeling is mutual. It tips her momentarily off balance. Though this Carly is obviously from Dani's side of the church, she has a vulnerability that Dani can see clearly, behind the bravado. Even the way she is standing so close to her brother. Dani knows if she can see it, the others will sense it and that is dangerous. The weaker Carly seems, the stronger the others will feel. They'll want to perform to get the reaction. Each will want to feel it is his actions that have exposed the chink. Dani never shows any chink in her armour. She doesn't need to. She's got Trevor on her left, Sonny on her right, a truck full of Stanley knives and twenty fucking soldiers around the corner.

"Let's get on with it." Trevor is not usually softly spoken but he says this quietly. It has the effect of calling the Meet to order.

There are fourteen of them in the small workshop and it's starting to warm up, yet it still smells like the damp cavern it is. Everyone takes a seat around the large makeshift conference table. The five seated to Dani's right are known in Hackney as the Lincoln Court boys. It's where they grew up. Four are related, John, Carly, Whisky and Tony Devon, who now has his foot in a plaster cast. The other two, Simon and Abdi, she knows are their friends from childhood. Dani's met most of them before and they are usually OK. In fact, she knows Trevor has sometimes had dealings with Whisky, the oldest. They have used her before because Tony is a repeat customer. They know the play. They know how this is supposed to work.

Carly perches on the lip of her chair, first putting her elbows up on the table, then removing them and interlocking her hands on her lap. Dani smirks inwardly. She looks left to the Holly Street boys. She knows Jason has a reputation for being hot-headed. She glances over, scanning him quickly.

His dress sense is, at first sight, unremarkable. It's just like most other eighteen year olds, the baggy jeans and designer top, diamond on a pendant around his neck and gold on his fingers. She checks each item of information off in her head. What does it mean?

Phillip now tells her it is Jason who instigated the attack on Tony after seeing him leaving the flat of Jason's former girlfriend, Jeanette.

"She ain't with him no more." Tony stares defiantly across the table. "She gave him his walking papers."

Jason's nostrils flare. "Yeah? Come round again. We'll see who's walking."

"I don't need to, mate. She comes to me," boasts Tony.

"We'll see."

"Yeah we will. Where d'you think she is now?"

Jason sits back in his chair.

"Alright." He's nodding, ominously.

Dani interjects impatiently.

"Look, I ain't no fucking agony aunt. OK?" She addresses Jason. "What you want today?"

"I don't want nothing." Jason points across the table. "I've only come here today to tell him he's gonna get hurt if he keeps taking the piss with me, but he's going on bad cos he's got people with him." He shrugs theatrically. "I'll just wait till I see him by himself."

Dani indicates Whisky to Jason.

"So you wanna war with these guys?"

He shrugs again.

"My boys'll back me."

"So you're gonna war over a girl?"

"It ain't over a girl!"

"What's it over then?"

"I just fucking told ya."

"No you never. You told me about some girl business."

Dani keeps her tone level. "I'm just tryna understand if you're saying you wanna war over her, whether she wants you or not."

Tony sniggers, pleased with himself. Dani's brow descends as she turns to face him. She glimpses Carly's eyes, wide with excitement.

"Is she with you now, Tony?"

He nods, smirking.

"Did she see you run?"

He looks uncertain.

"She saw you getting chased?"

"Yeah."

"Then she called you after?"

He frowns.

"I called her."

"The same day?"

"Yeah."

"Why didn't she call you?"

He glares now, his eyes flickering to Jason.

"What did she say?"

He juts out his chin.

"To come and get her, innit?"

"And you went and got her?" Dani's voice is quiet.

Tony is shifting in his seat.

"Did you go or did someone else have to go for ya?"

Now it's Jason's turn to sneer as Dani's brow descends even further.

"So what the fuck you grinning at?"

Tony smoulders as Dani turns back to Jason.

"Assuming she's gone …"

"It ain't up to him!"

"Yeah but it's up to her, ain't it?"

Jason says nothing. Dani knows exactly what type of man he is. Her gaze settles on him.

"Well ain't it?"

They sit, staring at each other. Dani's expression has returned to equanimity, while Jason breathes noticeably through his nostrils. When she blinks, her eyes remain shut for a moment longer, as if allowing her brain extra time to process. When they open again they settle back comfortably into gazing into his. Around the table no one moves. Jason breaks it first, leaning forward in his seat.

"Danielle. This boy here's taking the piss. He stabbed up my bredren and everything." He indicates Owen at the end of the table who has bandages running from his neck, across his chest and up his back.

"Yeah?" Tony has found his voice again. "You lot set a fucking dog on me! What did you want me to do?"

Dani is still watching Jason. He has called her by her full name, drawing out the pronunciation for maximum effect. No one calls her that. Her mother has always said her name was chosen before she was born. Even when her parents were angry and would call her siblings by their full names, she remained Dani.

"You think we're just gonna let that go?" Jason is defiant. "Owen's got a chipped collar-bone, you know! So come on, Danielle. Do your thing. Don't fucking sit there looking at me for a clue. Sort him out!"

She blinks again but she doesn't bite. Instead she continues deciphering what she can see in front of her. Jason's gold tooth shines, as his lip curls, but Dani cannot be distracted now she has locked on to her target. The room is silent as she continues her appraisal.

Sonny sits on her right. His thumb is the only part of

him that moves. He sends a text. "One car." His texts mirror his speech. Darren is in the Wessex Arms. He finishes his drink and gets to his feet. He nods to the others who follow suit. Trevor is sat back in his chair on her left, his elbows on each armrest. His hands are clasped across his stomach with his head tilted back. His eyes are far away, appearing to be focused on the brickwork above.

Dani's jaw is clenched now as her eyes travel first to Jason's hair. His dreadlocks are unkempt, the sizes varying around his head until they reach the right side by his ear. Here they are neater, tighter. His eyes are bloodshot from smoking too much weed, but they are also yellow where they ought to be white. His gold tooth stands apart from the others like an after-thought, shining along with the diamond pendant around his neck. Dani blinks again, looking now at his clothes. His top is plain black with a small designer motif on the cuff and his jeans are baggy like the young kids wear. Finally she looks down at the enormous, bright lime green trainers. She blinks once more.

She can feel those around her starting to fidget. Jason lets out a derisory snort. He has only agreed to come here today because the youth worker will tell his probation officer of his cooperation. It might just keep him out of jail when he returns for sentencing. He actually has no intention of abiding by any agreement made tonight. He sucks his teeth and laughs. He wants to make it clear he's unimpressed. He looks around at his boys.

"Gotcha", she says to herself. That, to Dani, is a tell.

"You wanna know what I see?" She speaks gently, quietly, glancing up again at the locks on the side of his head. "You're right handed."

He adopts a bored expression, clearly unimpressed.

"Most people start their locks in a hairdresser's so they're in neat rows at the beginning. Yours ain't like that cos you did them yourself. You did them in jail so obviously you've done proper sentences, twos and threes – years, not months."

His chest rises ever so slightly as the sneer returns.

"A couple of those would make you older than most of these guys." She nods in their direction. "But you still dress like you're eighteen."

His smile falters.

"You smoke a lot but it's the drink that makes you kick off."

Now it's his turn to stare.

"The drink helps you do the things you wanna do but it's also the reason you keep getting caught. It makes you reckless." Her expression conceals just how much she is enjoying herself.

"That top you're wearing, it doesn't match the rest of your clothes. That's cos you never bought it. Jeanette bought it. She bought you clothes and she looked after you." Now she leans forward, dropping her voice. "Maybe you should have chosen her over the drink."

His temples begin to pulse as Dani continues.

"You see, getting them is one thing, keeping them is another. Like doing crime innit? You can commit the fucking act but that don't mean shit if you can't get away with it does it? There's no point if you have to do bird every other fucking move you make is there? Them diamonds you're wearing are more expensive than people realise, ain't they?"

She holds up a hand, counting off fingers. "They've cost money, girls, time …"

She can see he's getting riled.

"Every time you get out you're on probation or you're on

licence, but you just can't keep yourself quiet cos you're tryna catch up on what you've missed. So you're on it double time. You drink hard, smoke hard, graft hard and anytime your girl asks if you remember all the stuff you said when you were inside you just box back another drink, leave the yard and do something worse than you did the day before."

She can see him heating up. She only has one more question that needs an answer. She wants to know who has seniority amongst his boys, but she doesn't want to make it obvious. She suspects now that it's not him. If it had been, he wouldn't have sought their approval when trying to insult her. He's made her decision for her.

She's gonna settle this by separating him from the others. Then she's going to get inside the head of the most senior of his boys. She's gonna use his own people to convince him he's no longer interested in the girl, because it's this dispute which has potential to escalate. She's here to stop the cancer. That's what they're paying her for. She moves in her seat, effectively blocking Tony from Jason's view. She isn't going to involve him in the discussion at all. Nothing Tony's gonna say will help.

She throws out a line. "How long was he with her?" addressing her question to the chubby youth sat next to Jason. He hesitates, caught off guard. He glances at one of the others and then shrugs before answering.

"Couple months."

Her smile is sudden and unexpected. "What's your name again? George?"

"Yeah."

She looks at him a while, nodding. This is just for show. She's really interested in the one George looked at before answering. She can feel that Jason is pissed off, but before he can say anything she looks to the leader she has just ferreted out and says," So not long then?"

"Nah, not really." His bald head shines and his short sleeved shirt is straining at the bulk of his biceps. He fancies himself, this one. "But at the end of the day yeah …"

Jason's pissed off.

"Am I fucking invisible now? You can't fucking ask me? I didn't call you bitch, did I? Or Whore? I called you by your fucking name!" He's shouting now. "I told you it ain't about the girl."

Dani knows he's behaving like that out of embarrassment. "What's it about then?"

She also knows that Sonny is sending a further text. Four of the soldiers in the bar around the corner pay for their drinks and go to their car. They will drive up and park at the end of the road. It's not the shouting, but Dani's response that makes Sonny do that. He can pick up things in her tone that others can't.

Dani looks around the table, evaluating everyone's reaction to the shouting. She clenches her jaw at Carly who, despite her poker face, is nervously shrinking back into her chair. She shoves the image out of her head, instead looking at the boys that Jason has claimed will fight for him. George is biting at the nail on his little finger while another sits on his hands. They are all watching Jason except the bald headed leader whose eyes meet hers, evenly. He will stand by Jason in any war. The others will only do so reluctantly.

Her eyes travel around the table, resting back on Jason who's glaring at her now. She can tell he is used to getting what he wants when his temper kicks in. He's not really bothered about his friend's stabbing. His pride is hurt about losing this girl and he's reacting to the way Dani has trivialised the relationship.

She looks straight at him. She can't show any weakness by acknowledging his insults.

"I'm talking to your guy cos he's thinking about compensation for Owen. You're still going on about this girl."

She's hoping the leader will say something, but he doesn't. She can't look at him right now, but she would really like to gauge what's going on in his head. Is he the real leader or does Jason's temper veto that? She's about to find out.

Jason glances at Trevor whose gaze appears not to have left the ceiling. He knows he is being watched because people tend to look at him when they're thinking of burying their fists in Dani's face. Trevor remains motionless.

Dani digs at Jason again, indicating Tony.

"If she wants the lover not the fighter, that's the end of the argument innit?" She spreads her hands. "So you need to let that go so we can talk about what you can get."

Jason's eyes close down and Dani takes the opportunity to look at Whisky. A quick shake of the head tells him to remain quiet. He understands. He moves back in his chair hoping his boys pick up the signal. It would help if Tony would take that fucking smirk off his face. Dani can hear Sonny's thumb tapping at his phone again. Everyone is moving in close, parking up, tooling up. Dani glances over at Carly. She looks uncomfortable. Good, Dani thinks grimly. Maybe next time, you'll stay home. This ain't a fucking spectator sport.

She hears the engine of Mikey's truck pulling up, nearby. It's time to go for the final pressure valve on Jason's nerves.

"Cards on the table. Are we talking a love thing here?" She wants it to sound as lame as possible, yet she asks as if

Dani smiles.

"If you get cash you either piss it up the wall or buy gear to make more cash. You've gotta split your cash with your spar Owen, innit? So you'd have the hassle of buying a smaller amount of gear. Whenever you get money you weren't expecting you gotta be smart and invest it don't ya?"

He nods slowly, appraising her.

"How do I know he's gonna pay?"

Dani smiles, lopsided.

"The fact that I'm here means he has to."

Jason sneers.

"What you gonna do if he don't?"

Dani points a thumb over her right shoulder.

"That's his department."

Trevor is leaning against the doorframe of the workshop, watching them intently. Jason looks back at her with grudging respect.

"Why's he standing there?"

Dani smiles again.

"You can ask him if you'd like."

Jason takes another look over at Trevor.

"I want three ounces then."

She nods back.

"Sounds about right. It's pure profit, going straight in your pockets and he'll be paying while you're earning."

He smirks at the thought of that. Dani knows she's broken through.

"And you'll forget the girl?"

He looks mistrustful.

"He can't come fucking bowling around Holly Street with her!"

"Don't worry 'bout that. I'll talk to him. Sweet?"

"I want it brought straight to me and I want it kept quiet."
Their eyes meet. "I don't want no fool hearing about it and tryna rob me."

"Yeah. Sure." Dani nods, holding his gaze. They both know he's not giving poor Owen a bean.

He grins now like he's won some major victory. He's convincing himself of that when he walks back to the arch.

"Yeah, we're cutting out."

He smiles to his own crew and gives Tony a smirk before he leaves. George, the leader and the others are looking confused. Dani smiles for the second time, shaking each of their hands, thanking them for coming, telling them it was nice to meet them.

They wait in silence till they are sure both of the cars have driven away. Dani holds up three fingers to Whisky. He'll be pleased. He was expecting to have to give four. Tony starts laughing. She gives him a look. Nothing fucking funny about that. She wonders if she should have a word with him. Maybe get Trevor to do it. She decides against it, as she doesn't like hanging around once a Meet is done. Get paid, get everyone out safely and move on.

Whisky adds their money to that left by the other boys and hands it to Trevor. He's still pissed off about the three ounces, cos he's the one that will have to put it up front. He's looking at Tony in a way that tells Dani they need to leave.

Phillip has been waiting outside. He shakes her hand.

"Is it all sorted?"

She moves her head from side to side.

"Just a coupla bits and bobs to iron out."

She smiles. "Shouldn't be a problem anymore." The smile falls away when she sees Carly watching her. She turns away and gets into her car. Whisky comes over to the passenger side, as she is about to pull away. She presses the window release.

"Yeah. Nice nice," Whisky grins. "Listen I might have something else for ya. I got some geezers over West London I wanna do a bit of business with, but a couple of them look kinda …"

She cuts him off, nodding towards Sonny's reversing Range Rover.

"What's Trevor say?"

He smiles.

"I never really had a chance to run it by him. I just want you to have a look at them. Scope them out for me."

She shakes her head.

"Talk to him first, OK?" She raises a hand before he has a chance to continue. Changing the subject she asks, "What was Tony doing hanging around Holly Street?"

Whisky shakes his head ruefully.

"Jeanette brought him there."

She raises an eyebrow.

"She musta known Jason was gonna kick off."

"Tony's been telling her he ain't scared of no one and all that."

Dani smirks. "Bet he never told her about today."

Whisky makes a face.

"He's on the phone to her, now."

Dani has a sharp intake of breath.

"Fucking hell. Is he into her?"

Whisky nods.

"She's staying at his place now. Couple of us had to go

down there to get her stuff. It nearly set the whole thing off again."

Dani looks up at him. She can see how worried he is.

"He ain't got no reason to go back has he?"

He shrugs.

"Well he better not cos I just agreed he'd stay away."

"When were you gonna tell me that?"

"I had to give him something, didn't I? He weren't happy about losing Jeanette."

Whisky looks back at Tony who is still grinning.

"I'm gonna spend my life dragging that boy outa scrapes."

Dani laughs, looking skywards.

"Talk to Trevor about that other thing. Take it easy, yeah."

The window goes up as she drives off.

She's deep in thought on the way up to north London. She always replays these events in her head. Today was tricky, but she prefers it that way. She's dealt with many people who, unlike Jason, have no intention of going to war with anyone. They're just cowards really. It's easier to send a load of threats and then call a Meet so they never have to back them up. She sighs. The problem is you never know that until it's too late. The next time that happens she's just gonna get up and give them her "this is beneath me look" before saying: "Come on Son, Trev. This ain't for us." She finds those so unsatisfying. They're just a big let down, a farce. It makes a mockery of all the mental preparation, the ritual and superstition.

The real ones really get her going. The Meets when something big is at stake, usually money. When she gets called to stop real violence, the type that leaves a permanent mark, then she feels good. She loves the thrill of the edgy atmosphere, the drama. All eyes on her as she feels her way into their minds, manipulating and cajoling, the attrition of the bargaining as it stretches into the early hours. She never crumbles. She doesn't smile too much and never makes a throw away comment. There's no such thing. Today wasn't bad but she likes to come out mentally drained. Instead she's a little wired. That can be dangerous for her.

She thinks back to the first negotiation she ever did. It was a far cry from today's meticulously organised summit. In the beginning she worked on pure instinct. Now there is a somewhat choreographed element to her approach. Experience has taught her that certain mistakes cannot be made twice …

That night she'd taken a short cut through the Broadwater Farm estate, on the way home. She always walked with her head down and her hands shoved deep in the pockets of her jeans. As she turned yet another greying concrete corner, she heard shouting. It was unmistakable, the barking of angry fired-up young boys.

The escalating tension had drawn her in like a magnet. She was nosy and could never resist adding her ten pence worth. She had an opinion on everything. As she drew nearer to the crowd she saw that as she'd expected, she recognised some faces. They had a boy surrounded. Dani knew his uncle. She took her half-smoked spliff from behind her ear and lit it as she approached.

"What's going on?" Her tone was one of mild curiosity. One or two of the boys gave her hostile looks. Who the fuck was she? She should mind her own business. Terry looked nervously at her from the midst of the angry mob. One boy peeled away, walking towards her.

"Alright Dani?"

She'd dropped him home from a party in a stolen car once. She nodded, blowing thick blue smoke from her nostrils.

"What you saying, Shaun?" She inclined her head towards Terry. "What's he done?"

"Him and his boys robbed Wayne's brother." Shaun indicated a stocky white boy with a close shaven head.

The boys waited, unsure if they should attack in front of a witness.

"Yeah? What they take?"

"Two ounces."

She raised an eyebrow as she looked at Terry. Idiot.

"How d'you know it was him?"

Wayne was one of the boys nearest to Terry. He leaned across and boxed him hard on the side of the head.

"Cos he's here trying to sell it back to us – in the same fucking wrapping!"

Terry was hunched over, holding his head. Dani glanced skyward. She sighed, looking at Terry.

"Is that all of it?"

Terry glared.

"Come on! You want me to leave you here?" The other boys were looking at her now. She turned to Shaun, speaking in a low voice. "Right now, I can't leave him. He's my little cousin."

It wasn't true, but then again, with black people someone only needs to know your parents to qualify as family. The rights that come with that include administering discipline and saving their arses.

"I don't give a fuck." Wayne was agitating.

Dani talked fast. "Yeah but you want your gear back innit?"

"They've smoked nearly all of it. This is only half an ounce."

"Don't matter. He owes you." Dani gave Terry a withering look. "People pay their debts, they don't get hurt, innit?"

Terry looked horrified, Dani remembered. He had no intention of paying back anything. She addressed the group.

"How long you gonna give him to pay it all back?"

"Till tomorrow," said one.

"One hour," said another.

"Don't be silly, now." Dani looked at Wayne. "If you don't want it back, don't fuck about. Just give him a kicking now and I'll carry him home."

They looked at each other, clearly disgruntled. They'd had more than just a beating in mind. They'd planned to leave a more permanent message for his friends. Dani was well aware of that, she'd seen the glint of steel in amongst the crowd when she first approached.

"Alright, listen. Give him three days. He's gotta go sort it out with his boys. If he don't come back by Monday midnight, with your other one and a half ounces, you can do him and I'll keep walking."

The boys looked disappointed. Dani talked with the cocky impatience of a time-share salesman. "Look, it's a lot less headache to you lot to get the gear back, innit? Otherwise you're after him, people are after you ..." She waved her arm in a circular motion. "That shit can just go on and on like Ariston."

"Na man! Who the fuck's she?" The smallest of the group was almost hopping up and down with anticipation. Dani looked the imp up and down.

"Who'd ya buy the gear from?"

The imp piped down, staring round for the answer. He had no idea. He'd just come along for the excitement. Dani smirked. Empty barrels always make the loudest noise.

He threw a hand up in her direction. "What we listening to some girl for?"

Dani fired back her answer, flicking the end of her spliff at him.

"Cos I know who you get your gear from." (She didn't). "If they find out you've been turned over, they could just turn up and start asking for their money now. You bought it on tick, didn't ya?"

There was no reply. Outwardly her expression was grim. Inwardly she was delighted. It was only a guess but she knew young boys had no qualms about taking chances like that. She was having fun.

"I don't need to tell you how them people operate. They got a chance to strong you up now, innit? You don't wanna owe people like that. They'll have you doing all sorts. You like mugging old ladies?"

She could feel the anger coming off them. It was not the same anger she saw when she arrived. This was fear. "Look. If it was me, I'd want the gear back." She threw another dirty look in Terry's direction. "With interest. That way you've given Terry a warning and you come out on top."

She looked to Shaun for an answer. He wore all designer labels as usual. He preferred money to violence. He nodded. She arranged a time for them to meet again.

"Go on Terry. Go home."

She didn't even turn to look at him as he stepped carefully from within the group. But it wasn't all smooth. Once Terry had left, the boys, sensing they'd missed an opportunity, made a number of threats but she managed to talk them round, distracting them with talk of possible drug deals. She sat and had a smoke with the group before leaving. She remembers the way she felt as she headed home. What if Terry didn't pay them back? She should have minded her own business.

It was a good thing she knew Trevor …

They all meet up at Omonia in Hornsey. It's a Cypriot pool club Dani's been going to since she was sixteen. Charlie, who owns it, has also known her since they were at school together, though they only became friends years later.

He was one of the first people she told she was gay.

At the time the club had belonged to one of his uncles. Dani and Charlie had both been attending the local college and were part of a large group of friends. They'd gatecrashed a party that night and following all the fights, arguments and young love break-ups that happen at teenage parties, they met up at Omonia.

They'd been lounging on a sofa doing the "we will always be spars, I love you man" talk, when she admitted to liking his cousin, Helen. What cemented their friendship (after he stopped laughing) was he kept that information to himself and never treated her any differently. He himself had lost his job and his wife and children due to an horrendous gambling addiction. His family gave him the club as part of his recovery process and he'd managed to keep it going.

Charlie lets them use an upstairs room to sort out their money and as usual some of them would stay, have a drink and shoot some pool. Only she, Trevor and Sonny remained tonight.

The atmosphere at Omonia was a total flat line to the younger soldiers, so they never hung around for long. For the first time that day, she could finally relax.

The club hasn't changed much since she first started coming here. It's on the ground floor on the high street. The lower two thirds of the glass front is frosted and the cream-colour vertical blinds are permanently closed. The sign on the window says "members only".

If a non-member walks in he will see mostly elderly Greek Cypriots drinking coffee and playing Kalooki. There will be a number of younger men of varying nationalities, usually playing pool. Dani would be the only female he'd be likely to see in there. As a non-member, he'd feel as if he'd inadvertently walked into someone's living room. He'd probably turn around and leave.

Sonny is out in the back yard, smoking again. He's speaking to his wife, checking on their three kids. She's not his wife but they've been together since he was seventeen – seven years. And he's not speaking. He's listening. He leans his tall wiry frame against the wall as he smiles at today's funny stories and takes the shopping list. Nappies, wet wipes, formula …

Trevor and Dani are playing pool. She's relaxed now so she's running her mouth, trying to put him off his game. It works with some people, not him. "Why you taking that shot? Take the easy one … always trying it." She sighs. He doesn't answer. "This is why you're gonna miss that shot, because you're trying too hard. I think it physically hurts you to lose to me. Is it because it happens so …"

He makes the shot anyway. She kisses her teeth theatrically while he clears the table, grinning. She racks up again.

She winds most people up when she acts like this, but Trevor is not affected. He knows that she is always the same after a Meet, relieved, but mostly behaving in a way she can't during those meetings. She secretly believes that most of the time she is much cleverer than people around her realise. When she gets angry she has to use all her self-control not to make that clear, not to embarrass them into defeat and submission. She doesn't want to invite vengeful thoughts.

Trevor is suddenly serious. "Why d'you think Johnny brought his sister along?"

"Fuck knows. Bit simple that one."

"Yeah but she ain't."

"What d'you mean?"

"Well while you was sorting out all the shit, Sonny was watching her."

"Yeah? What was she doing?"

"Watching you."

"So?"

"So I don't think it's cos she fancied ya."

"What then?"

"Dunno but I'd give that one a wide if I were you."

"She didn't like me. I saw that."

"Exactly. So why come along?"

"Maybe she wanted to see me perform." Dani is smirking.

"Don't think so. Watch her." He's serious.

His phone rings. It's his wife, Paula. She's pissed off about something, so he's gonna make a move. "Call me if anything, yeah," and he's gone.

2

Marie

t's almost midnight when Dani leaves Charlie's. Sonny left
over an hour ago. She has the window down as she drives,
letting the breeze clear her head. She and Sonny seem
to have gotten through another eighth in the last couple of
hours. She'll smoke the end of her last one when she parks
up.

She's got Tanya Stevens on in the car. There's only one
way to play that, so she has to turn it down before entering
the road Marie lives on. She pulls up around the corner and
walks to the house, smoke swirling from her nose.

The light is on in the hallway. There's food in the kitchen.
Oxtail and rice, plaintain, avocado pear. There's carrot juice
in the fridge. She eats in front of the TV. She doesn't watch
the music channels because the women piss her off; instead
she puts in a sports video. Tonight it's a re-run of Michael
Jordan tearing up John Starks. She likes the way he taunts his
opponents. It makes him play even better. She likes watching
the other guy wasting his energy trying to think of a good
comeback. He has already lost. She used to behave like that
all the time because she's so competitive. Nowadays she has to

be diplomatic. She has to be careful not to let her frustration bubble over. Sometimes that can be an effort.

After that first time on the Farm, she was called on a few more times until it eventually became obvious she couldn't pick and choose who she spoke for, if she wanted to be seen as neutral. At times she was asked to help with disputes over stolen goods but refused to help negotiate drug deals involving class A gear. She didn't want her name associated with that.

She concentrated on gang disputes because she hated hearing some kid had been shot or shanked, and the guy who'd done it couldn't even remember why, by the time he was getting lifed off. Trevor came in almost immediately because she knew her manner was not always appreciated. She'd been threatened a few times and some even refused to pay, until he agreed to become a regular at her side. "Why not?" he'd said. "It's extra change."

Trevor and his wife Paula had gone to the same secondary school as Dani, though they were two years above her. She came to Trevor's notice one day during a fight with a boy from her class. Trevor ran over to join the circle of rowdy onlookers only to find that the one being held down on the floor was a girl. His outrage when he dragged the boy from her turned to amusement when she climbed to her feet, taking advantage of Trevor restraining her attacker, and punched him twice in the face, breaking his nose.

It's 2 a.m. when she finally decides to go to bed. She checks on Jessica, who is two. She always sleeps on her back, legs stretched out, arms flung over her head. A star. She's kicked the covers to the floor.

Dani smiles and covers her before turning out the nightlight and pulling the door to. If she wakes her making noises in the shower, she'll be a little bastard for the whole of the next day. She needs her sleep. She looks in on Marie, who's fast asleep. They have been together since Jess was nine months old.

Strangely, it was the news of Jessica's impending arrival that provoked the beginning of the end of the relationship between Marie and Jess' father, Lloyd. They'd been together for less than a year, but Lloyd was delighted. This would be his first child. He moved out of his brother's flat and in with Marie, looking forward to his new family.

But Marie felt she'd been taken for granted. They'd never spoken of commitment and she was alarmed at the ease with which Lloyd insinuated himself into her life. The more he got comfortable, the more Marie became irritated, forcing her to examine her feelings for him. From Lloyd's point of view, Dani's arrival on the scene could not have come at a worse time.

Marie and Dani met at a christening. Dani had to go because a close friend of her parents was related to the father. She hated going to those things. She'd have to endure endless questions about not being part of a couple, not having "a young man". She wasn't able to change the way she dressed even in the centre of West-Indian straight land. Her parents, to their credit, never added to the pressure. They saw her for who she was, but never felt the need to discuss it or bring it all out in the open. That would never happen.

Dani had been talking to one of her cousins when Marie approached, holding the baby. They were not introduced, but Marie noticed how Dani glanced at her a few times more than seemed necessary. Marie had been carrying the sleeping Jessica over her right shoulder. She awoke and began crying. She was surprisingly loud considering her size.

Marie tried unsuccessfully to change the baby's position but she was holding her drink in the other hand and began to get flustered, looking around, annoyed and embarrassed. Lloyd, tired of trying to please her, had spent most of the day smoking outside with his friends. She'd been arguing with him earlier but she at least expected him to help with Jess.

Dani's cousin had turned away as her name was called, so Dani held out her hands to help Marie, who made to give her the drink, saying 'thanks', but Dani gently took Jess. She turned her so she could see her face and held her up in the air.

"What's her name?"

"Jessica." Marie watched the smile form slowly on Dani's face as she looked at her daughter, saying softly, "So, Jesse. What's the problem, ah? You need a change of scenery? Yeah, me too."

Jessica stopped crying and pouted instead, distracted by the unfamiliar face.

"She likes you," said Marie, smiling too.

Dani was still smiling when she looked back at Marie, shifting Jessica to her right shoulder with ease and glancing around to see if anyone had noticed the way they were looking at each other. She'd been with enough straight women to know the signs, but she wondered if there was a daddy bear around.

When she looked back, Marie was gazing towards the exit doors again. Dani allowed her eyes to travel the length of Marie's body and back up to Marie's eyes and raised eyebrows. She'd sighed, trying to stop smiling. She couldn't.

"Well now Jesse. If I hold onto you, I'm less likely to get a slap from your ma. Think you can protect me, eh?"

Marie was taken aback by Dani's overt behaviour. Who does that?

"Her name is Jessica," she'd said firmly and held out her hands.

"OK, beautiful," said Dani, "Looks like I have to let you go for now."

She was looking at Marie as she spoke, but Marie liked to think she was a tough nut to crack. She told herself to stop smiling and walk away but Dani wasn't done.

"You know just before you took her back, Jesse here was giving me her number."

Marie's eyebrows were on the move again. "I didn't hear that."

"That's because she was whispering." Dani's eyes were roaming over her body.

"She doesn't have a number," Marie said, a little frostily.

Dani smiled. "Must have been yours then."

Marie had to laugh. "Really? What did she say?"

"079 … and then you interrupted."

Marie was still laughing as she walked away. Dani stole another look at her as she left. Stunning.

Had she given Dani her number then, she may not have got a call. Dani was all about the chase, so she spent the rest of the evening smiling whenever they caught each other's eye. Marie was at once flattered and incensed someone could be flirting with her so blatantly and Lloyd not even notice.

He says nothing. He's watched Dani go through a number of relationships just like this, a baby and a girlfriend who is independent – in that order. It always feels to him as though these are family units Dani can walk away from if she wants to, leaving them completely intact.

He knows that if he were to split up with Sita, it would rip apart two families who have been through so much to finally learn how to get along, not to mention what would happen with their children. No, he still loved his wife and couldn't imagine their family not being together.

The day was uneventful. As usual Sonny would take care of the finances and administration of the business. Dani had no head for figures and no patience for dialling endless phone numbers. Anyway, she hated talking to people on the phone. How are you supposed to know what they really mean when you can't see them?

She would spend the day with the staff. She knew all of them and would travel constantly in order to see them. She used this time to praise those progressing and to help those who weren't. It was also a time to get to know the employees she wanted as soldiers. Today she's asked Christian to go help one of her elderly customers clean out his shed.

"He needs help with the heavy lifting and stuff. Should take you a day but go back tomorrow if it's not finished."

Christian nods, saying nothing. Inside he's cursing. He's been working on a school's grounds with five other workers. They'd been having a good time, laughing and joking their ways through the days. Now he was gonna have to listen to some rickety old codger going on about the war.

Dani watches him closely, knowing exactly what he's

thinking.

"That alright, yeah?" She holds out the address.

"Yeah." He takes it without looking at her. "Who's gonna drop me off?"

She's walking away when she turns, "You won't need any tools. Take the bus."

He clenches his jaw, ignoring the enquiring looks from the others as he stalks out of the yard.

She heads back into the office. "Call Mr. Goldenberg. Tell him Christian should be there in half an hour."

Sonny nods.

She calls the old man at the end of the day.

"How're you feeling today, Mr. Goldenberg?"

"Oh I'm fine like thread. At my age it is a foolish waste of energy to complain."

She smiles. If he ever complained the sky would fall in. "So how was he?"

He chuckles. "Young people are so sullen these days."

"He wasn't rude, was he?"

Whether Christian knows it or not, today was a test and if he fails he'll never be a soldier.

"No no. Not rude, just sour. You young people lose your laughter so early these days."

Dani waits patiently while he drifts off mumbling to himself about the curiosities of the world, then he says, "There were no problems with him. He did everything I asked."

"Did you make him go back and forwards, you know, run him up and down?"

Again he's chuckling. "I believe I tried his patience but he stood up to it. The shed is quite clean, spotless in fact."

Dani nods, satisfied. "Good. Thanks for that."

"I'm afraid I can think of nothing else that my garden needs, Dani."

She laughs. "Oh don't you worry. We'll think of something. I'll see you soon OK? Take care."

"Try to do the same, Dani. Try to do the same."

She plans to go clubbing this evening. Clubbing for her is playing dominoes in the back of a gay nightclub. She just needs to spend time with her friends. Normally a number of her soldiers will pop in and check on her from time to time and some like to hang out there because of the atmosphere. She was secretly pleased at the way her boys reacted to seeing her on the gay scene; the way they just took it in their stride told her more about them than they realised. The ones that didn't like it just stayed away. She had no problem with that.

She could still remember the days when she'd have to sneak into secret doorways to get into gay venues.

After work she goes back to her own place. She calls Marie as she cooks.

"I'm going Sugar's tonight, babe."

"Oh, OK. What did Ian" (she refuses to call him Sonny) "say about Saturday?"

"They already have plans."

"Hmmm. OK."

"They do."

"Relax Dani, it's not a problem."

"What do you mean relax?" She's pissed off now.

"You don't have to defend him."

"I'm not defending him. Defending him for what?" Dani is raising her voice.

Marie is calm. "Look, I can accept that we don't get on, it's you that's always trying to push us together … Jess wants to talk to you."

Dani takes a deep breath. "Did she hear us arguing?"

Now Marie is irritated. "She heard you shouting but I wasn't arguing. I'm just telling you how it is."

Another deep breath.

"Daniiii." Marie has handed Jessica the phone, before walking away.

"What's happening, Jesse?"

"I playing my dolly Sarah."

"Yeah? What you doing to Sarah?"

"I brush her hair."

"You're brushing her hair? Does she look pretty like you?"

"No."

Dani laughs loud.

"I read you story tomorrow. Alright?"

"Yeah story morrow."

"OK then. Night Jesse."

"Ni night Dani."

Jess has put the phone on the floor and toddled off with her dolly. Dani is still smiling. She uses her shoulder to hold the phone to her ear until eventually Marie comes back on the line. She knows Dani will have temporarily forgotten her bad mood so she tries broaching a sensitive subject.

"Are you coming over tomorrow evening?"

"Yeah. I said I would."

"You don't have to come if you don't want to."

"Are you trying to piss me off?"

"No, I'm trying to be nice." Marie sighs.

"Yeah, how does that work?"

"I'm just saying Dani, that if being around my family is too much for you ..."

"Did I ever say that?"

It's Marie's turn to take a deep breath. There are times when what ought to be an easygoing relationship seems too much like hard work. She does her best to avoid arguments with Dani. She tries again.

"I want you to be there ..."

"Are you sure about that cos ...?"

"I *really* want you there, Dani, alright?" She is patient now, speaking firmly. "And you know Jess will want you there, I was just saying that if you're not in the mood for dealing with my family then I would understand."

"You want me to be there?"

Marie closes her eyes, counting to ten and exhaling slowly. She already has a child!

"Do you want to be there?"

Dani laughs. "No, but I'll come anyway."

"Tell me why you don't want to be there."

Dani pauses, choosing her words carefully.

"I don't enjoy watching your cousins, who are not actually related to you, pawing at you just to get a rise out of me."

"No one but you paws at me and if you come I'll make sure it stays that way. OK?"

Dani is chewing her lip, thinking about it. Marie adjusts her tone again.

"Do you want to come over after your club tonight? Shall I leave the light on?"

"Maybe."

"We'll be here if you do. Alright?" She's asking if the argument is done.

"Yeah, OK." Dani feels bad. She was over-reacting. She's

smiling now. "So I might see you later?"

"That's up to you." They're both smiling. Marie hangs up with a sigh of relief.

3

Venus

enus was in the Stoke Newington High Street, situated in the basement of one of those community cafes you only find in places like Hackney. As she walks down the stairs, Dani thinks about her earlier conversation with Marie. She doesn't want to be around that family any longer than she has to but feels she should be there, they've been together almost two years.

She knows it's obvious to Marie's family they're more than just friends, as Marie claims. She isn't all that bothered as she's experienced this reaction before, but it concerns her that even Marie's friends keep a frosty distance. She feels little Jess picks up on this and becomes reluctant to go to some of them, preferring to stay by Dani's side. This in turn pisses Marie off and she'll then deliberately create distance between Dani and Jess, scolding the toddler when she wants to sit on Dani's lap or have a cuddle.

Her thoughts are interrupted by her best friend Shelley, shouting across the room as she reaches the foot of the stairs.

"Dani Big Shot!"

She grins.

"Shelley Thunder!" she shouts back, her spirits instantly lifted.

She makes her way across and sees Shelley's girlfriend approaching from the left.

"Alright Lisa?"

"Hi Dani. Where's Marie?"

Dani pulls a face. "At home with Jess."

"There are such things as babysitters, you know."

She ignores that and sits down by her friend, elbowing her.

"Where's the victims?"

"At the bar."

They play dominoes any chance they can get. It's another opportunity for Dani to run her mouth. They all play that way, having learned from parents and older relatives that trash talking is a necessary part of the game. The dance floor is through black doors at the end of the room but Dani has no desire to venture in there, preferring to relax with her friends.

Angela and Debbie return from the bar to find Dani already shuffling dominoes with a gleam in her eye. They've all been friends since their days at college together.

Dani didn't have many friends at school. Having Trevor in her corner was a definite asset, but he was always with Paula. She'd found that time of her life quite difficult. Struggling with her sexuality, in love with her best friend of the time and fighting constantly. Laura was oblivious to her feelings and had boyfriend after boyfriend, while Dani burned with jealousy. Things came to a head one day when Dani, unable to keep a lid on her feelings anymore, snapped and attacked her as she walked her home one night.

Laura had been complaining about her latest waste of space boyfriend and then disclosed she'd recently lost her virginity to him. That incident ended their friendship and started the wave of inevitable rumours. Dani was devastated by her own behaviour and by the loss of her friend. She had no choice then but to finally accept who she was.

She was relieved to start college and leave her tortured school life behind. From the beginning she felt more confident. Her world had expanded. She made a few friends and disclosed her sexuality when she thought it appropriate. Shelley was out and proud and they took to each other immediately. Shelley introduced her to Angie and Debs, who were in a relationship at the time. Despite a break-up, they still remained inseparable as friends. The four of them had forged a solid unit since those days and watched each other's lives unfold without judgment. They liked to spend time together to recharge before going off into the world again.

Shelley doesn't ask about Marie. She likes her well enough but understands Dani doesn't want to bring her to gay clubs. They play dominoes through the night, shouting, insulting, teasing and laughing. The players change as Shelley leaves to spend time with Lisa, returning later. Angie and Deb alternate playing with dancing next door.

Dani, though, remains at the table, her boasting and ribbing constant. She notices one or two soldiers hanging around, which only adds to her feeling of invincibility. She's feeling good and decides she'll complete her night by going to Marie's later. She's now partnering a girl called Pat, playing against Angie and Debs.

The music from next door roars in her ears each time someone enters the games room. This time it's Sonny who walks in. She looks up. It's not unusual for him to check in on the way home so she gives him a wink and goes back to her game, assuming he'll make his way over to the pool table.

She slams a domino down on the table and looks up again. Sonny's standing behind her partner. She doesn't like to cheat but she never misses an opportunity to test her mind reading skills. She wonders if she can work out what's the correct play even on his poker face. Instead she notices Sonny appears unsettled – worried in some way. She's had a few beers by now so she figures he's concerned about her driving home. He's always a bit of a worrier.

"Gonna wait for me, son? It's the least you can do seeing as I've ended up talking myself into going to Marie's thing on my own."

"Yeah, you ready now?"

"Behave! Can't you see I'm kicking ass here? Relax. Shoot some pool. It's early."

He glances towards the dance room. When he looks back at Dani she's watching him, sobering up. Something's wrong. The roar again from the dance room and Shelley and Lisa are approaching, hand in hand. Lisa notices the way Dani and Sonny are staring at each other and says, "You told her then?"

Everyone looks at Sonny. The atmosphere's changed. He flashes a look of warning to Lisa and turns back to Dani.

"I'll tell you in the car."

When he first walked up to her, she had a stupid grin on her face and a spliff hanging out of the side of her mouth. Now she's alert and serious. This isn't the first time he's told her to leave somewhere for her own safety, so she gets up. She turns to Shelley to apologise before leaving, but they're all getting up with her. She figures she'll hear why in the car.

They pile into his Range Rover and she asks, "So what's going on?"

He's fumbling with the keys, in a hurry to get the car started.

"What? Tell me."

No one will let him out in the traffic.

"Tell me now." This time she's said it quietly.

He sighs. She's not gonna let him stall any longer.

"It's Susanna."

She freezes. She can't breathe. "What's happened? Is she …?"

"No. No, she's fine."

"What then?"

She's looking around at everyone in the car, while Sonny is trying frantically to get the car out into the moving traffic. Then the penny drops. She says nothing, although she's livid. She opens the car door and steps out without a backward glance, walking straight back to the club.

She marches past the door staff wordlessly and heads down the stairs. She walks into the dark dance area and begins circling the outer corners. Where else would Susanna be? Probably with the rest of the fucking crack heads. She's muttering this type of thing to herself as she looks for the bunch of druggies with Susanna in the middle. A hand is on her shoulder. "I'm here."

Dani turns, half expecting to see one of the bouncers, unhappy at the manner in which she re-entered the club. It's her. It's Susanna – and she looks well. In fact, she looks beautiful. She's lost most of the signs of the cocaine addiction that was beginning to take hold the last time they were together. She's smiling, head tilted to the side, and Dani feels eighteen again. It's that smile. She wilts under the heat of it ...

Sonny is seriously pissed off. He doesn't think it'll do any good to go after Dani, back into the club, so following Shelley's suggestion, he agrees to drop them all home. The problem is that Lisa's going home to her own place tonight and she's the last drop-off. So now he's listening to her talking incessantly about Dani. She knows just enough from pillow talk with Shelley, that he can't help but listen.

It had been Lisa that first spotted Susanna in the club and pointed her out to Shelley. She, in turn, had become anxious when it was clear Susanna was looking for their friend. Shelley advised Sonny to get Dani out of the club as soon as he could. He hadn't asked why. He knew Dani had some sort of weak spot for the addict Susanna who used to steal from her. He'd assumed Dani was trying to help her with the addiction. This wasn't the story he was hearing now.

"Apparently, it was love at first sight on Dani's part," Lisa begins. "She was infatuated because Susanna was straight, older and sophisticated. Then they start seeing each other and it turns out that Dani's not the pussycat Susanna was expecting. So they have this intense love me, fuck me, jealousy thing going on which ends up with Susanna addicted to drugs and Dani strung out and addicted to Susanna, until Dani becomes part of the reason for the addiction or something like that." Lisa draws breath. "Then they realise they *really* love each other, but can't be together because Susanna brings out the worst in Dani, which as you know is not very pleasant." Sonny bristles at this, but Lisa adds, "And Dani brings the worst out in Susanna, which is *killing* her. But every time Susanna starts a new relationship, back she comes to Dani, they fuck and re-run the whole break up thing over again."

Sonny is wishing she would shut her fucking lying mouth. He's sure Dani is always faithful but also has a nagging feeling some of what Lisa's saying could be true. He can't get her out of the car fast enough when they arrive at her place, because he wants to call Dani – mostly to reassure himself that she is going home to Marie tonight.

But she's not answering her phone … maybe she's still in the club. He actually knew very little about the Dani and Susanna relationship. He never asked about it and Dani never mentioned her. He assumed they broke up because of Dani's attitude to hard drugs.

There was one occasion when Susanna appeared at a party and Trevor told him in no uncertain terms to "get Dani the fuck out of here now!" No one really spoke about it but yet it seemed to be common knowledge Susanna's reappearance always spelt trouble for Dani.

Sonny frowns as he climbs into bed. Sita rolls over, throwing an arm across his chest.

"You alright?"

"Hmm."

He doesn't tell her because he knows exactly what she will say.

"Sonny, she can preach it but you actually practise it."

He closes his eyes.

4

Susanna

"You look good," says Dani, stomach churning.

Susanna's still smiling.

"How are you, Dani?"

"I'm good. You?"

"I'm OK – more than OK. How are the troops?"

Another smile from Susanna, then, "How's your regular?"

Dani smirks.

"Be nice." It's her turn. "Who are *you* here with?"

She's looking around, trying to fight the acrid jealousy rising in her stomach now. The rage of it makes her feel sick. She's thinking Susanna must have come here with her latest girlfriend.

"Just me and Sophie." Her best friend.

"OK." She's relieved – and it's obvious.

Susanna looks down at the floor. "I came to see you, actually. Can we go somewhere?"

Dani has also been looking mostly at the floor, not trusting herself to gaze at Susanna for too long. Her eyes now blaze with shock and hope, but Susanna says, "To talk ... I need to talk to you."

Dani smiles sheepishly.

"Oh. Yeah, OK."

"Can we go somewhere public?"

Dani's smile dies.

"Just for a coffee," Susanna adds quickly.

"Alright, but I can't drive. I've been drinking."

"I'll drive."

"You got a car now?"

"No, Dani. You have." They both laugh, trying and failing to avoid each other's eyes.

"Come on then."

Susanna sits at the table watching Dani at the counter. She smiles, shaking her head. She knows Dani is explaining how Susanna's coffee needs to be, strong, sweet and hot. Dani's hair has recently been cut. Susanna tears her eyes away from the nape of her neck, just as she turns to head for their table.

Dani places the drinks in front of her.

"I got you these."

She produces chocolate biscuits from her jacket pocket.

"I don't know if you're hungry ..."

Susanna smiles. "Why would I be hungry, now?"

Dani's jaw clenches. Susanna looks down at the table.

"I'm sorry. I – I ..."

Dani's look is searing.

"I just meant ..." She shakes her head. It doesn't matter.

They sit in uncomfortable silence. Susanna is looking out of the window chewing her lip while Dani just stares at her that way she does. Her hair has grown since they were last together. She looks like she did when they first met. Now Dani is looking at her skirt. It's white, cotton against her dark skin. They should be going on a picnic. It makes her look innocent and carefree. She is also wearing a short cardigan type thing over a top. Dani can see she's dressed like this so as not to provoke her, as if that's all it takes. It's no wonder she didn't blend into the crowd inside the club. She looks vulnerable. Dani wants to fuck her.

This is the first time they have seen each other in almost a year. To Susanna it feels longer. She finds herself wondering if Dani has outgrown her.

"I'm seeing someone."

Dani's visibly disappointed. Susanna's always seeing someone, but it never fails to hurt when she hears it.

"You don't need to announce it to me do ya? Unless you wanna tell me who she is."

There's a hint of menace in her tone. She's even more disappointed because she knows there must be a specific reason for Susanna's announcement.

Susanna can see Dani clearly now. She hasn't changed at all. She realises she can't do this here. It's harder than she thought it would be. When she went over it last night with her girlfriend, it had seemed much simpler.

"Can we go to your place please?"

She's holding her forehead, getting upset. Dani is thinking the girlfriend probably needs sorting out for some reason.

"Yeah OK, we can walk from here."

They're now walking in an uncomfortable silence, enough room between them for another person. Dani is remembering the last time they met. Being alone with Susanna always puts her on edge.

When they walk into the flat, Susanna stops, close to the wall. Close to the door. She's remembering the last time she was here. Dani stops down the hallway. She turns.

"Come on, I'll get you something to drink."

Susanna hesitates. She's not going any further.

"I'm clean now. I have been for nearly a year."

Dani looks at her, smiling.

"That's great, Suse."

She walks towards her as Susanna winces at the use of the pet name.

Dani's holding her breath. Is this the time when they finally start thinking of being together? She'll miss Jess. This is what she's thinking when she realises Susanna is still talking.

"… And I've been with my girlfriend for eight months."

No response as Dani tries to work out if she's had sex with her during this relationship, probably not. She is trying to stop herself thinking this way when she is suddenly, violently yanked back to reality. Did Susanna just say 'baby'?

Dani's hand is suddenly on Susanna's stomach. She shrinks back against the wall at the expression of horror on Dani's face, trying to hold herself together.

"No, no." She pushes Dani's hand away. "I'm not pregnant."

She's annoyed that Dani still acts like she belongs to her.

"Not yet, I'm – I'm …" She slaps at Dani's arm in an effort to stop herself from stammering. "I'm planning to …"

"What!"

Dani's incredulous. It's the last thing she'd expect Susanna to say to her.

"With who?" she snarls. "Who is she? No. Susanna, you can't do that!" She's frantic. "Have you lost your fucking mind?"

"Dani …"

"Fucking try it!"

The polite girl saying please and thank you in the coffee

shop is cast off like an ill-fitting cloak. The old Dani has made a swift return.

"Dani, please. I want …"

"No. You go on, Suse. You fucking try and see what I do to her." She's shouting now.

Susanna looks away, chewing the inside of her cheek.

"I'll fucking find her. You know I will."

"Stop it!"

Dani comes close, pointing in her face.

"I'll break her hands! I'll break her fucking legs! Go ahead. You wanna be a single mum? You fucking try it, Suse. See what I do …"

"Please, stop."

It's almost a whisper as Dani breathes heavily, penning her into the corner. Susanna lifts her head, "Dani, you know I love you … but it's time for me to move forward. I need this," she pleads. "Please calm down. Please."

Dani's hand is back on her stomach. She is struggling to regain control of herself. She takes a deep breath through her nostrils to calm the violent shakes that are breaking out along with hot panic-induced sweat.

They wait, Dani's eyes closed. Susanna is watching her patiently until she opens her eyes slowly.

"You want a baby?" She speaks softly now.

"You know that." She lifts her hand and strokes Dani's cheek.

She feels Dani's hand slide up her body, between her breasts. She is pushed back against the wall. Dani moves in closer.

"Who you gonna have that baby with, Suse? Who is it that don't know you're mine?"

She's talking quietly, directly into her ear. Daring her

to say it. Susanna turns her head to look directly at Dani. Sometimes she'd like to smash her face in with a hammer ...

"What are you going to do, Dani? Live in two households, raise my baby on the side and your regular's on weekdays?"

She's heard about Dani's girlfriend having a baby. Dani kisses her cheek.

"What's your girlfriend's name?"

Susanna knows her too well to answer that.

"What's yours?" Susanna kisses Dani's lips, staring at her.

"You know *her* name. Who is she?" Dani kisses her this time.

No answer again.

"She send you here to tell me this?"

They're talking quietly now, almost whispering.

"She knows I'm with you."

A long kiss. A breath.

"Does she now?"

When Dani kisses her this time, it's just the way Susanna likes it. Intrusive, invasive, consuming.

"What time is she expecting you back?"

Dani's hands are moving now. Stroking her back, cupping her breasts. Susanna's arms creep around her neck.

"You're such a bastard, Dani. You know that?"

Her top is lifted to reveal her bra. Dani has trouble with clasps at the back. She smiles when she sees the clasp to the front. She takes Susanna's hands, walking backwards, leading her to the bedroom. Susanna is biting her bottom lip.

Dani is whispering in her ear as her fingers slide in and out.

"I miss you. Why d'you make me wait so long? I can't be without you. You know that."

Her own breathing is becoming ragged, as Susanna gasps for air.

"You trying to leave me Suse?"

"No, baby."

"Who is she?"

"Look at me, Dani." She knows her. She knows if she doesn't stop her, she'll get angry. "I love you, Dani. You know I love you."

They stare at each other until Susanna begins to go over the edge. She digs her nails in, raking them down Dani's back as she comes, moaning, panting for breath. She bites down on Dani's shoulder as the last shudder racks her body.

Marie wakes groggy and disoriented. She's left all the lights on in the house and Dani is still not home. The clock by her bed says it's almost four in the morning and she knows the club finishes at two. She climbs out of bed trying not to stomp too loudly round the house as she turns out the lights. She hates it when people say one thing and do another.

Susanna wakes to Dani's weight pressing her down. She kisses her forehead before craning her neck to look at the clock radio. It's ten past five in the morning. The sun is about to rise. It will be another hot day. She kisses her again, letting her head sink back into the pillow. She lies deep in thought, unsmiling as she strokes Dani's neck.

This is the fourth time they have slept together during Dani's relationship with Marie. She knows Dani would never tell any of her friends that, definitely not Sonny.

She has always allowed herself to be overwhelmed by Dani's thirst-like need of her. She knows she's addicted to that. She wonders if Dani's girlfriend ever sees what she sees.

She believes Dani does not – cannot love that woman. She's a little concerned Dani has stayed with this one for so long, her "regular" as she calls her. The jealousy between them will always be there. Oddly, she finds it comforting. She shudders at the thought of the day Dani finally gives up on her. Even her announcement last night didn't do it.

She knows she's seen the worst of her. In her opinion, the person she loves is the real Dani. She knows Dani would think nothing of having her girlfriend bundled into a van and threatened – or worse. Dani's soldiers are not the Merry Men of Sherwood Forest. Her therapist at the rehab centre has warned her of the dangers of being around Dani. He told her the risk of relapse if things go wrong between them. If she's honest, she'd have to say she knew before she left home this afternoon that this would happen.

She carefully rolls Dani off her before climbing silently out of bed. When she returns from the bathroom, she sits on the side of the bed as she dresses. It's getting light outside. She stares down at Dani's face. She looks satisfied, peaceful.

Susanna shakes her head grimly, before gathering her things and leaving.

5

The Morning After

Dani wakes slowly, opening one eye at a time.

"Suse?"

She sits up in the bed suddenly wide-awake. Instinctively, she knows she's alone and bends forward as if punched in the gut. She heads for the kitchen, looking for Susanna. They'd normally shower, get dressed and go to the local cafe to have breakfast, where they could gaze at each other intently, touching under the table and whispering promises.

She'd thought about their having a baby together last night in between the bouts of lovemaking. There had been no angry fucking last night. She hasn't given a moment's thought to the girlfriend because last night confirmed she didn't count. But then – where's Susanna?

🐾

In the shower, Dani's back is stinging as the water hits. She checks in the mirror to see the evidence. She'll have to stay away from Marie until she heals. This isn't good. She dresses in a long sleeved shirt to hide the marks. There are a number of missed calls on her phone so she scrolls through looking for an unfamiliar number. It's mostly Sonny. Now she remembers yesterday. Fuck! She's always tried to keep him away from Susanna. To have both in the same room is to be two different people. She certainly doesn't want Sonny to know they've slept together.

She needs to find Susanna. She wants to know who her fucking girlfriend is. It doesn't occur to her to call Marie. There are many things about Marie that appeal to her, her independence, her looks, her dignity. There is more, but she is not Susanna. Susanna loves Dani – and Dani knows that's never in question. With Susanna there is no need for self-monitoring. She will love her anyway. She's seen Dani in action when she was at her most uncontrollable.

Marie would never stay with her after seeing her stamp on someone's hand for touching her.

Marie would never tolerate her pushing her up against a wall at her workplace because she missed her and needed her now.

It's not as if Susanna likes this part of her, it's more that she sees the fear and weakness that drives that type of behaviour. She knows Dani's ashamed of that side of herself and tries to fight it. Tries to be a better person.

Normally she'd get Trevor to find out stuff, find people. Or she could get Sonny to put one of the soldiers on it. She can't ask either of them to do that here. The soldiers are only ever asked to do things that would help during negotiations or keep someone safe. Traipsing after the love of her life is not in their remit.

She's mulling this over as she drives to Sonny's house. She

pulls up a couple of streets away and makes a call. It rings a long time before it's answered.

"Fucking 'ell! I thought you'd dropped off the face of the earth. What you saying Dani?"

"What you saying Anton?"

"Every ting! Long time no see."

"Yeah I know, how's work?"

He's a former soldier who now works as an electrical engineer.

"Good. What can I do for ya?"

"Nothing. How's that cousin of yours?"

"Who, Dennis? He's just got out again, the mug! He's not hearing, that one."

"Where's he at now?"

"Staying at his mum's yard, eating her out of house and home."

"What was he in for, if you don't mind me asking?"

"ABH. He attacked his boss at Macky Ds."

She laughs. "Sorry. Look, I got a bit of work for him. Just for me on the quiet, whaddya reckon?"

"Shall I get him to call Sonny then?"

Sneaky little fucker. That's his way of asking "how quiet?" She's silent, waiting for the correct response.

"I'll text you his number."

"Just give it me now." That quiet you nosy bastard. She writes it down. "How's Stephen?" His boss. "I've been meaning to give him a call." Dani knows Anton is secretly sleeping with his boss's daughter.

"Yeah he's good. I'll tell him you said hi."

"Nice one. Thanks for that, Anton. Speak to you soon."

"Yeah. Take it easy." He's trying to work out if that was a threat about Stephen. You never can tell with that lot, especially Dani.

She hangs up. She'd have felt bad about the threat if her head wasn't completely screwed up about finding Susanna. She calls Dennis immediately and arranges for him to travel down from Oxford.

This is definitely not the way they usually recruit. There's nothing about Dennis that says he's right for them apart from the fact he's been begging to be a soldier for as long as he's been aware of their existence. She's confident he'll be eager to please. He'll try his hardest. She can meet him at the station and give him the photo she carries hidden in the back of her wallet. She also has addresses of all the rehab centres around London, places Susanna used to live and work ...

First, she has to face Sonny.

"What's up, babies!"

The house is chaos as usual. Sita smiles as she opens the door. Dani says, "You alright, Sweets?"

She can tell he's said something to Sita. Fuck. Sonny tells her everything. It took Marie almost a year to find out where Dani lived.

She's playing with the kids when he comes into the kitchen. He has a spliff in his hand, ready to light, so she follows him out to the garden. She's not gonna apologise, so she builds her own while he smokes. He's surly.

"Abdi's grades are shit." He doesn't want to talk about Susanna. Good.

"What's he studying again?" She inhales deeply. He gives her a look. She knows all of the employees.

"Computer installation at Barnet Tech."

She considers his tone. They've always maintained some

boundaries, largely due to the difference in age. She'll let
that one go.

"What are his grades?"

"Two Ds."

"Out of?"

"Seven, but he's gotta pass all of them."

"What are the others?"

"Cs, one B. Not good enough. Thinks he's a soldier now."

"I'll talk to him."

He nods. Silence.

"You gonna call Marie, then?"

She's sitting at the garden table. He is standing to her left,
slightly behind her.

She sets her jaw, turning slowly to look at him. She lets
the expression on her face sink in before she speaks.

"Call Marie for what?"

"Well you obviously didn't go home last night otherwise
you'd have answered my calls." He's standing his ground.

"Did you fuck your wife last night, Ian?" Her voice is
low, simmering with rage. "Oh I'm sorry, that's none of my
business." She stands up suddenly. She's in his face in a flash,
pointing at him.

"Don't you ever fucking talk to me about my personal life
again." She turns and walks into the kitchen, the smile back
on her face. "See you later babies!" She knows she can't fool
Sita so she doesn't try.

Sita picks up their baby son Cameron, and walks out into the
garden. She can watch the girls eating from there.

"What happened?" Dani and Sonny have their moments
but it's unusual for her to walk out without breakfast.

Sonny sits smoking. She can't tell if he's angry or hurt.

She knows how he feels about Dani – she can do no wrong, normally.

"Did you ask her about last night?" Sita sits down with the baby.

"She wasn't very happy about that."

He can't bring himself to say he thinks she's cheating on Marie. Sita says it for him.

"She must have strong feelings for this girl."

He shakes his head. "Dani wouldn't do that."

"Maybe she did go home last night."

"She would've answered her phone. She never ignores my calls. Never."

He pulls his son onto his lap. "Dani hates people who cheat. She's even sacked a couple of people just cos she didn't like the way they handled their business. I don't get it. I must be missing something. There's no way she'd be having it with anyone like Susanna."

"She might have kicked it. It's been a while."

"Yeah, but she's stolen from her and everything. Dani may be soft but she wouldn't lower herself."

"But what if she actually cares about her, babe? Maybe she can't help it."

"This is Dani we're talking about, Sweets."

She puts her arms around Sonny because she knows the truth. He obviously didn't notice the blood seeping through the back of Dani's shirt.

Dani drives straight to the yard, looking for Abdi. He is about to get into the truck, bound for Leyton. She tells him to wait in her office while she speaks to Darren, his crew leader and one of her button men. He confirms Abdi's a hard worker, reliable and punctual.

The office is in fact an oversized shed. There's gardening equipment lining the walls, some new, some for repair, some for the knackers' yard. Two large desks face each other with piles of paperwork in trays. Both she and Sonny are tidy and organised, so there's little mess.

Sonny's chair is bigger than hers. She moves it to the side of the desk and takes her own, moving it round the side also. She needs to see what Abdi does with his hands. Are his legs restless? Where does he look when there's nowhere to hide? She points him to Sonny's chair with a smile.

"You're not in any trouble, I just want to check in with you. See how you're getting on."

She smiles at him again. He's nervous. His left arm is tight to his side, his thumbnail digging into his overalls at the thigh.

"How are you finding the job?"

"Yeah, it's great, I love it."

She laughs, genuinely pleased at his answer. "OK, tell me what you love most about it."

"I like feeling my hands in the soil." She is taken aback by that. She looks at him intently, turning the full force of her bullshit detector onto him.

"What do you hate most about it?"

"Mowing lawns, cos it's boring."

He's passed with flying colours, a little less tense now. Here goes.

"How's college?"

He shifts in the oversized chair.

"It's alright." His voice is flat now, head bowed.

"No love?" She bends forward to look up at him. He's quiet. Avoiding eye contact, looking at his boots.

"*Anything* you love about it?"

"Well, not love but the man dem are alright."

"In your class?"

"Yeah they're alright."

"Hate?"

"Most of the lecturers."

"What are they like?"

"Lazy!" He looks up now, indignant. "You ask them anything they tell you it's in the book, but sometimes you don't get what the book is saying. That's what they're there for innit?"

"What are the good lecturers like?"

"They stay after so you can ask them if you don't get it."

"What are your grades like?"

Now he's squirming. " They could be better?"

"Don't ask me," she says quickly and he gets that worried look back as she adds, "Look. I'm gonna tell you what's happening in your life, right now."

He's very worried now.

"Your good grades are the ones where you rate the lecturers. The reason you rate the lecturers is they don't allow you and your friends to treat their classes like a social club. So you actually learn shit. You talk in the other classes cos you figure they're not gonna help you anyway so fuck it, right?" She doesn't give him time to respond.

"But what you gotta understand is you need to get good grades even if all the lecturers are shit. You have to figure out a way to get your questions answered. Ask yourself this. How come you are good at the subjects that you like the lecturers for? If you think about it that must mean you have the ability to be good at all the subjects. Imagine that! Once you understand that, take a step further and ask yourself another: Will I accept a lazy bastard of a teacher deciding what I can and can't be good at? Once you get your head round that you'll find a way to be disciplined enough to save your socialising till after the class is done."

He's silent, but he's nodding.

"Where do you go when you're not working?"

"The mosque. Home."

"Anywhere else?"

"My mum's not very well."

"You the oldest?"

He nods.

"Once a week you'll go out with the boys, it'll go down as overtime, but when you're in college, you study. OK?"

"You not gonna sack me?"

"Not if your grades improve. I know you take responsibility for your family, now you're gonna take responsibility for your studies. Deal?"

He smiles.

"Deal."

"You got a girl?"

This time it's a shy smile.

"Can she get out?"

"If you write her a letter." He's grinning. She can see the child he was. Cute. Cheeky before he got things to worry about.

"How old?"

"Nineteen."

She gives him a crooked smile, impressed. His girlfriend's a year older than him. Susanna is four years older than Dani.

"You treat her right?"

"Yeah! But I don't want her around the sol- ... the boys."

"How long you been with her?"

"Year and a half."

"Fair enough. Take today off, paid. Relax, new start tomorrow."

"Thanks, boss."

"Dani."

He can't say it but he's still smiling.

Sonny walks in. She glances at him as Abdi is leaving.

"Wait a sec, Abdi. Why computers if you like gardening?"

"My uncle needs me to join his business."

She nods, watching him. He waits now, unsure. Dani smiles.

"We'll see you tomorrow." She smiles again as he turns to leave.

Sonny moves his chair back to his desk and sits. She's feeling bad about earlier and now she wants to talk with him about Abdi, who she thinks is a sweetie. She saw no resentment in him when he spoke of the family business. He obviously has a sense of duty. He just needs to be allowed to blow off steam from time to time. Sonny can help her with him.

She looks across at him. He is already on the phone, avoiding her. He knows she'll be watching him. When he puts the phone down she says, "Look, I can't talk to you about last night OK?"

He looks across at her, shocked. "You're not saying it's true!" He can't help himself.

"I'm not saying anything!" Fucking hell! What is it with this guy? She can feel she's gonna lose it again if he doesn't mind his own fucking business.

"I need to talk to you about Abdi."

He is staring at her, his temples pulsing.

"Are you ready?" She's abrupt. "Can we get some work done?"

"What about him?"

Now he's fucking sulking. She ignores this and proceeds to tell him her thoughts.

She does her best to show him how much she needs his input. He knows that already, but it's the only way she can make it up to him because she cannot give him what he wants.

They eventually manage to thrash out a programme of support for Abdi, despite the frosty atmosphere across the table.

It's lunchtime.

"Wanna get some food, Son?'

"Oh we're back to Son now, are we?" He can't stop himself.

Their eyes lock for a moment before she stands without a word and leaves. Who the fuck does he think he's talking to? She turns the music up in the car as she drives out of the yard, pretending she hasn't heard her name called. She heads up the high road, cursing under the sound of the music.

If it wasn't for his mum, he wouldn't be here getting on her fucking nerves, taking the fucking piss. Dani wouldn't have been able to pick Sonny out from a line up! He was just another one of the boys at the youth club she worked in at the time.

She spits chewing gum angrily out of the car window, knowing that wasn't quite the truth. She had noticed he was one of the few white boys that hung around with black kids but saw no reason to try and act like them.

His mother had stopped her in the street one day and during

the conversation declared that Sonny trusted Dani with his life. She'd been visiting him regularly while he was in custody awaiting trial for a robbery. He protested his innocence throughout, despite what appeared to be overwhelming evidence. Dani had made it clear from the outset she believed him. Sonny was no angel, but she knew this wasn't his style. She was the one who drove the family home from court on the day the case was thrown out.

His mother's words had made a big impression on Dani. She had not felt she'd given him special treatment at the time. She'd advised him on occasion when he found himself in scrapes with the police. She had spoken to him about his girlfriend when they had problems, describing how she believed he should behave towards her. Dani did remember telling him she was proud of him when he refused to join the bullying of a young boy on his estate.

But it was only after the conversation with his mother that Dani began to understand how influential she was in his life. She watched him for a while after that. She saw the way he matched his morality to her own, yet remained independent. He was no attention seeker, but he relished her guidance. He soaked up her declarations and opinions and seemed to make them his own. There were others in the youth club that she was fond of, but in Sonny she saw someone who truly had the potential to be a special person.

Like most boys his age, trouble found Sonny on more than one occasion, despite his attempts to avoid it. She recalled it had been a Thursday evening when he paged her. She was at home. Her girlfriend was out and Dani was on baby-sitting duty. She was watching snooker with little Josh sleeping on her stomach. She'd been too stoned to put him to bed.

Sonny didn't sound right when she called him. He'd asked what she was up to, as if they were friends. She guessed something was very wrong but didn't tell him to come over. She knew all types of people but gave very few her address. It may have been different if she lived alone. She asked if he wanted to meet her on an industrial estate in Edmonton and the way he agreed, the speed of it, made her leave little Joshua with a neighbour.

When she arrived she saw he was in shock, one side of his T-shirt covered in blood. He'd found his older sister bloodied and beaten by her boyfriend and attacked him with a hammer. He had no idea how the boyfriend was, but remembered hitting him so hard that a tooth had pierced his upper lip. She checked his mini-van and saw the blood inside it. She was vaguely aware of comments she'd made to him in the past about what should happen to men who beat their girlfriends, but in truth she would have helped him anyway.

She'd taken his clothing from him down to his shorts and burned it all in a barrel by a breakers' yard. She'd found water in another rusty red barrel and made him wash himself down. Together, they emptied his van, broke the windows, dented the doors, smashed the lights and removed the licence-plates. The breakers would, with any luck, just wheel it in their yard next the morning. Sonny could report it stolen in a couple of days.

Finally, she took him home, gave him a tracksuit and forced him to watch the rest of the snooker, while they smoked and drank through the night. They didn't talk about the beating.

He, in typical Sonny fashion, was not forthcoming and she wanted to know as little as possible. What was obvious was that Sonny had an even temper, but if you pressed the wrong buttons, he could detonate. Properly. There was a part of her that liked that.

Dani's girlfriend had come home drunk. Dani took her to bed, allowing Sonny to sneak out and catch a cab back home.

When he was arrested the next day, he stated he'd been with his girlfriend all evening watching the snooker. Sonny added that whoever had beaten the guy had also had a go at his sister, because she, too, was black and blue. The police suddenly lost interest in the case and he was released on bail. The charges were eventually dropped. His sister's boyfriend, who'd suffered a pierced upper lip, a broken jaw and cheekbone and concussion, was too afraid to pursue the matter. Dani had sent Trevor and Mikey to visit him on his discharge from hospital. That may also have influenced his decision.

After that Dani became an honorary member of Sonny's family. Those who knew them well saw the bond but only his family knew why. There were other such incidents with members of the youth club who also became loyal to her for one reason or another but her bond with Sonny was by far the strongest. She'd been there at the most vulnerable moments in his life and her actions made her stand out from the other youth workers and adults in his life. Oh he had plenty of adults around him willing to fill the void the untimely death of his father had left, but they all talked. Just talk. Worse than that, they expected him to join in with their incessant jawing. Dani's less talk more action approach switched on a light in him that no one else had. And she understood his complete trust in her. She knew he had put his life in her hands, and so she guessed correctly that she in turn could trust him with hers.

Dani sighed as she crawled along in the mid morning traffic her temper had driven her to. Sonny could be an annoying little bastard when he was ready. Always repeating back stuff she said. "But you said this! You said that!'

Just because she knows right from wrong doesn't mean she expects him, herself or anyone else for that matter to be able to live by it! It's only half the battle won, knowing it! Who can be that fucking perfect?

6

Sweets

I n her car, she calls Dennis. She'd only set him up an hour or two earlier, meeting him straight off the train.

"Progress report, please."

He doesn't know her well enough to pick up the edge in her voice.

"Well, what it is right, I plotted up outside the Priory all morning, but nuffin. I'm going back there after I've eaten."

She holds her breath. She's upset enough people today.

"What if she turns up now?"

"She's gonna take at least an hour if she does. I'll be back before that, but the thing is that's the long way of doing it. What I thought was better was if I plotted up at the benefits office where she last signed on, for a week. She'll show up sooner or later, won't she?"

Fair enough. Might be alright this kid.

"Fine. Keep in touch."

She really wanted an excuse to have a go at him. Where is Susanna? She can't face Sonny, so she decides to take the rest of the day off. She misses Jess, but she can't risk Marie seeing her back. She should call, but this time she can't find the separation she usually feels after seeing Susanna.

She's not sure where to go or what to do. She's hungry so she drives towards home and goes to the local café. She should have had breakfast here that morning, with Susanna. She asks the waitress if she's seen her, but they've not been there together recently enough for the girl to remember who Dani means.

She finished eating and went to her flat, but found she couldn't stay there. She could almost feel Susanna had been there. She drove around for three hours. She went to the place where Susanna used to live. Nothing. She went to her old workplace. One of the girls remembered her and threatened to call the police if she didn't leave. She tried to find Sophie's place. No joy. Eventually she gave up and went to Charlie's. She called Trevor, who said he'd stop by after work. She spent the rest of the day drinking with Charlie, until Trevor turned up.

She's quiet as she plays pool. Trevor and Charlie exchange looks before Charlie sneaks out the back to call Sonny. By the time he arrives, she's well on the way to being drunk.

"Why'd you let her drink so much?" he hisses at Charlie, who just shrugs his shoulders. Sonny worries too much. Dani doesn't often drink, so maybe she needs to let her hair down today.

She's glad to see him so she stops mid shot to come over and speak to him.

"I'm sorry OK."

Sonny keeps his expression neutral. "It's cool. It's covered."

"You two been fighting again?" Trevor shakes his head, tut-tutting.

"We've got woman trouble," she says, laughing.

Trevor raises his eyebrow. Sonny shifts uncomfortably. It's bad enough she may be playing around but he certainly doesn't want her admitting it in public.

"You want answers now?" Her smile is rueful.

Sonny shakes his head hurriedly. "Na. Leave it."

"No, come on. I'll be honest."

Trevor is rolling his eyes "You gonna take your shot or what, Dani?"

She turns back to the table and bends over the cue, muttering.

"Truth is Son, she fucking drives me nuts. It's true. I can't help it, and before you say it I don't know *how* to say no when she comes around." She looks directly at him. "Then she fucks off again."

She pots and walks around the table. She looks at him again before taking the next shot. "Now I gotta pick up with Marie again."

Neither Trevor nor Charlie is usually the least bit interested in her love life, but both are surprised at what they're hearing. Trevor looks at Sonny, searchingly. He prays she's not talking about that Susanna. She is nothing but a prison magnet.

"It's cool, Dani. Don't worry about it. Come on, I'll drop you round Marie's."

Sonny's anxious to get her out of there. The last thing he needs is for any of the boys to turn up now.

"Hold up, Sonny," says Trevor. "We're playing a game here!"

"She needs to go home." Sonny looks intently at Trevor, pleading with his eyes.

"Forget it, mate." Dani says, "I gotta give that a wide for a coupla days."

Sonny's eyebrows knit in confusion as Dani adds, "Don't worry about it."

But she misses her shot and Trevor, finally acknowledging that something's not right, clears the table quickly and calls it a night.

Sonny takes her to his home. She's continued drinking and talking all the way home so he sets her up in the spare room, leaves a glass of water by her bed.

Sita is awake when he gets into bed beside her.

"Sorry, Sweets. Did we wake you?"

"It's OK. Is that her?"

He exhales loudly. "Spare room."

"Is she fully dressed?"

"Yeah! What?"

"Nothing"

"What, Sweets?"

"She might need a T shirt or something."

"She'll live."

"You're really pissed off with her, aren't you?"

He rises up on his elbow. His eyes have yet to adjust to the darkness.

"She's not even denying it."

"Babe, she's an adult."

He lies back down.

"This ain't who we are. We don't do shit like this." Despite his fury he is whispering.

"No, Sonny. It's not who you are. You don't all have a collective conscience. You are a good person because you're a good person. She makes her choices like everyone else."

"Yeah, but we don't get them choices. You know why she

sacked Darryl, don't ya? And now I find out she's being seeing this fucking druggie on the side. All that stuff she goes on about … we don't do this, we're better than that … Fucking joke!"

Sita puts her arms around him. She's always thought this day would come. Sonny grew up idolising Dani for no good reason that she could see. Yes, she helped him out, but that's what friends do. Big deal! Now the time had arrived, she wanted him to accept it, accept Dani wasn't infallible. She knew he was already trying to find excuses for her.

"Her back was bleeding." She says this quietly, tentatively. "I saw it this morning. I think they're scratches."

He doesn't speak, but even in the darkness she can see the anger and disgust on his face.

Dani wakes the next morning at six because Cameron is screaming for his bottle. Eyes still shut, she grabs the top of her head. Why is it thumping like that? Her ex, Sarah, sometimes came down from Bristol to stay at Dani's for the weekend, allowing Dani to spend time with Josh who was now twelve. Josh had a baby sister and maybe it's the baby the noise is coming from.

It's the fact she's still in her clothes that brings her back to reality. She opens her eyes and finds herself in the second to last place she wants to be.

"Shit." She needs to get out of there.

She sits up too quickly on the bed. Dani is no drinker. She stands, moving more slowly now, looking around for her shoes. Not there, so she tiptoes downstairs to the kitchen, where she walks straight into Sita.

"There's juice in the fridge … I won't be a minute." She has the baby's bottle.

"No I'm alright, I've gotta make a move."

Dani avoids eye contact, looking for her shoes.

"I just want a quick word," Sita tests the milk on her arm. "I'll only be a minute."

Shit! That's the last thing she needs. Where are my fucking shoes?

She goes to the living room. They're in there. She's trying to struggle into them without bending her head forward, when Sita comes in with a glass of juice.

"Thanks."

"What are you doing, Dani?"

She stops fighting with her left shoe.

"I don't know." She's deflated, collapsing back in the chair. "Is he awake?"

"You can't just avoid each other. Anyway, you pretty much told him everything last night," Sita says quietly, now giving Cameron his bottle.

Dani groans, cursing.

"Have you seen Marie?"

"I'm – I'm gonna call her today." She fidgets nervously with the sleeve of her crumpled shirt.

"What are you gonna say, Dani? Are you gonna tell her the truth?"

Silence.

"Dani. You can't keep lying to her, it's not right. You know that."

No answer. She's scratching at the back of her neck, avoiding eye contact.

"Have you hit your head or something?" Sita's alarmed. "What's wrong with you?"

Dani mumbles. "She's not gonna let me see Jess."

"Well, that's what happens when you play around."

"I'm not playing around."

"No? What do you call it then?"

She bows her head, trying and failing to smooth out the creases in her trousers.

"Come on Dani, this isn't Sonny you're talking to."

"What's that supposed to mean?" She looks up sharply.

"He thinks you're some sort of teacher or something. Fuck knows why, but he does."

Dani winces, bowing her head again as Sita continues, mercilessly.

"It's not so much Sonny, but what about the rest of them? It wasn't enough for you to help them out when they were down and give them a job was it? No. You had to get them at their most vulnerable and start indoctrinating them with the flipping 'Dani Philosophy on Life'!"

"It's only her." Her voice is small.

"It's only her, what?" Sita fires back.

Dani closes her eyes, exhaling loudly. "It's only her …" She can't finish the sentence.

Sita is incredulous.

"Oh well, that's all right then." She sighs. "Dani, they look up to you. They believe in the things you say because you were smart enough to reward them with success every time they followed you." She eyes her gravely. "Now they'll do anything for you, won't they?"

Dani looks up darkly. Sita's pointing at her now.

"Don't take it for granted. Other people don't have what you have because they didn't spend years cultivating it. And trust me, it can all be broken down in a day. You need to think carefully. If you lose Sonny and them, what will you be left with?"

Dani is searching for the right words.

"It's not like I've really been playing … it's just her."

"Why?"

Silence. Dani's holding her thumping head with both hands, but Sita is still relentless.

"Didn't she steal from you once?"

"Yeah, but it wasn't like that."

"Drugs?"

She nods, watching Sita closely.

"She doesn't really seem your type, Dani."

"She's clean now."

"How do you know?"

"She is."

"I thought you loved Marie?"

"So did I." She shrugs. "Then Susanna turns up." She looks at the ceiling. "And I forget."

Sita can't hide her disgust. "What if Sonny said that to you?"

"He'd never cheat on you."

"Oh yeah, why not?"

"Cos he loves you, you love him …" Dani waves her hand to indicate the home, the life they have built together.

"Sonny thinks it's because of what *you* taught him. He doesn't understand he was that person before you came along and told him who he should be."

Dani exhales again, feeling helpless. She's had enough of this.

"What else, Sweets? Since you've decided to kick fuck out of me, get on with it."

Sita puts Cameron down for his nap on the sofa and continues to do just that.

"He's so disappointed in you. So hurt. You better not let

the rest of them find out."

"So I gotta forget about her to please everyone else?"

"No Dani! You've got to be who you say you are!"

"I am." Her voice is barely audible now.

"Yeah – until you're really tested. And you've just given in at the first temptation. It *means* something, what you've taught these guys. They're not all like Sonny."

"I know. I know, I just …"

"What happened?"

The front door slams as Sonny leaves. Dani puts her head in her hands.

"He fucking hates me now. See that's what it is about Susanna. No matter what I do, she loves me anyway."

"Oh come on! That's not fair. You've been lying to him. It's like you've cheated him. He trusts you. He always has."

"I know that. I have tried, you know."

"Tried what?"

"Staying away from her. It's her that comes looking for me."

"So she turns up when she feels like it. You should tell her to fuck off! You have a life now."

Dani swallows.

"I don't wanna tell her that."

"OK - if she cares about you why does she leave?"

"You'll have to ask her that one."

"Got yourself in a right mess, haven't you?"

Dani nods miserably.

"She left in the middle of the night, Sweets. "

"Not before taking half your back with her."

She looks embarrassed.

"Yeah. That's a first."

Sita has a thought.

"Is she the reason you split up with Sarah?"

Dani grimaces. It's all coming out now.

"S'pose."

"And Dianne?"

"Sort of. She's always there ... Somewhere." Dani is looking out of the window, her eyes betraying her.

"So, where does she live?"

"With her girlfriend probably."

"Don't you care?"

"About what?"

Dani looks at her hard, daring her to say it. Sita carries on anyway.

"That she has sex with someone else and then comes to you when she's bored of it?"

"No, I don't care." Her voice is granite.

"What do you mean you don't care?"

"Cos she's mine." Dani's defiant now.

"How is she yours?"

She holds her pounding head again. "Ask her."

"I'd love to!" Sita snaps. "I'd love to ask what it is she does that has you abandoning every principle you ever had."

"Let me know when you find out."

"Do you think it's OK, what you're doing?"

"No, course I don't."

Silence. Then Dani laughs, ruefully.

"You know this is one of them things I always told Sonny to never let happen to him."

"What?"

"Sleeping on someone's sofa cos you've been caught out."

"Well, you haven't exactly been caught."

"The whole fucking club saw me leave with her the other night! I didn't even try to hide it." She shakes her head sadly.

"I ain't tryna hurt no one but I can't think straight when I see her. And I can't go anywhere near Marie like this." She points with her thumb, to her own shoulder.

"Nice of her to do that before running off back to her girlfriend, eh?"

"I don't know why she did that. Run off I mean."

"Great. Sonny thinks you can do no wrong and you think she can do no wrong."

"I do feel bad about it." Dani looks directly at her now. "I know it's wrong."

"Maybe you need to call it a day with her. Properly."

"No! I don't wanna."

"Then sort it out, Dani."

"I can't even fucking find her!"

"You know what I don't get?"

"What?"

"You have this whole other life that none of us know anything about, but you know all about us. I mean, how long has this been going on with this girl?"

Dani is chewing at her lip. She feels awful and getting a going over from Sita is not helping. She actually likes Sita, she knows she's right, but she would love to just get up and go. She stays because she doesn't know where else to go. She doesn't want to go home, she can't see Marie or Jess and she can't face Sonny.

"How long, Dani? How long with Susanna?"

"Always." It's almost a whisper.

"What do you mean? Not since you split up in college?"

Dani nods, looking up at her.

"You've been seeing her since then?" Sita's mouth drops open. "No way!"

"It's not … sometimes I don't see her for ages."

"Why?"

"Why what?"

"Why would you keep this up for what … twelve years?"

"She just …"

"What? Steals your money, ruins your relationships?"

"It's not like that."

"Oh yeah, I forgot. You ruin hers too." Sita shakes her head. "I think you need to be honest with Sonny."

"We don't talk about that stuff."

"Well, maybe you should, then your relationship could be a bit more equal."

"It is equal." Dani is shocked.

"No. It's not. That's what I mean. You know everything about him and he knows nothing about you."

"Come on, Sweets. He knows loads about me. So do you!"

"Not the stuff that matters, obviously."

"I can't tell him that stuff."

"But it's the truth isn't it? You love her but you can't have her so you cheat on your girlfriend."

Dani winces once more. "I don't think he's gonna trust me again."

"Well the cat's out of bag now. You need to front him up."

Dani looks fearful suddenly. "What if he don't want nothing to do with me when I tell him?"

Sita smiles gently. "He'll be OK. He brought you home last night, didn't he? Just be honest. That's what you always say."

Dani rubs at the top of her head.

Sita smiles again. "Why don't you have a shower, I'll make you something to eat."

"No, I better go home. I've got some calls to make." She stands, swaying unsteadily.

"Whoa! Sit down." Sita jumps up, guiding her back down into her seat. "You're not driving in that state, I'll get Sonny to call one of the boys to pick you up."

"No. No, I'm alright."

"Are you crazy? Do you know what he would do to me if I let you drive today? Go on. Bathroom. You'll feel better."

An hour later Dani's showered and is eating while she waits for Mikey, her driver for the day, to arrive.

"You're right you know, Sweets." Dani is feeling a little better although she is not used to discussing her personal life. "I do still believe in what I say. It's just that I let it go when it comes to my Suse. Can't do that anymore."

"You might be able to work it out with Marie, you know."

"Naa, she's got too much pride. She won't forgive me. Why should she? I've broken the biggest promise I made to her. Anyway it wouldn't be right. I'd never give Suse up, even if she asked me to."

Sita nods.

"Well it's not great but it's honest. That sounds more like the Dani we know, doesn't it, gorgeous?"

She's bouncing her baby son on her knee. Dani smiles for the first time this morning. She holds out her hands to take him, but Mikey arrives, sounding the horn outside. Sita follows her to the door.

"Thanks, Sweets."

Sita smiles, " Just sort it out, OK?" She hugs her.

"Yeah, yeah. I will. I'm gonna call Sonny now."

7

The Meet

Wassup Mikey?"
"You tell me."
She wishes Sonny had sent someone else. He's
Trevor's best friend, and if he knows Susanna's back, then
Trevor must know. Trevor has probably sent him to keep an
eye on her.

Mikey is not one of the soldiers. He's twenty-nine years
old and studying for a Masters degree in construction
management. He already runs a building company, which
he has in his partner Derek's name. It's growing slowly – his
word, but steadily – Derek's word. He's involved in the Meets
because Trevor brought him in and they understand each
other. Also because he likes the money they all make doing
the Meets. Who wouldn't?

"Where to?"
"I need to pass by my place first."
She puts some music on and dials Marie's work number,
keeping her tone and expression neutral for Mikey's benefit.
"Didn't I tell you not to call me here?"
Marie is not happy. If Dani says she's coming over and

then fails to do so, this is normally the response. The absence of an immediate explanation is not helping.

"I know. Sorry, I need to talk to you."

"I'm busy right now."

"Can we meet?"

"I don't know when I'll be free. You'll have to call first." She's not gonna make this easy.

"Can I pick up Jess, then?"

"No."

"Fine." Dani is annoyed. Not only does she have to ask, but also she's been refused!

"I have to go now, I'm working. You can meet me after work at six." She says it as if what Dani does is not work.

"OK … I'll call you later."

But Marie has already hung up on "OK."

Dani looks out the car window. Susanna would never do that, she thinks to herself. She would cuss me off, tell me she's not having it, but she'd never give me frost. Dani can't deal with that. My Suse wouldn't use a baby against me either. Her mind turns to what she said last night. Dani is afraid. Afraid Susanna could have a baby with someone else. Afraid of what she'll do to the other person if that happens. She knows it's wrong to think this way, but she also knows her reasoning will leave her permanently if she ever sees a pregnant Susanna with someone else.

Mikey watches TV while she changes out of Sonny's top. Today is not a good day to be borrowing his clothes. She's due to meet the father of a prospective employee in Bristol. She has Mikey for the day, so she'll take advantage of that. Usually

Sonny would come with her but she thought it best they give each other some space. She calls him from the kitchen where Mikey can't hear.

"Village."

That's how he answers the phone. She thinks about how he sounds much older than twenty-two years, his voice sounding too deep for his tall wiry frame.

"I'm going Bristol. Want me to pick you up?"

"No, I got stuff to do."

"Listen. I'm meeting Marie after, but are you gonna be about later on?"

"Probably gonna take a bit of time, that."

"What?"

"Marie."

"Don't think so, Son."

No answer.

"I've got a bit more experience in this area than you."

"Oh yeah? What area's that then?"

"The pack your bags and fuck off area."

She hears him exhale as he laughs.

"Shall I call you when I'm done, yeah?"

"What's left of you. Might wanna keep hold of Mikey."

She grins. "I'll speak to you later, Son. OK?"

"Good luck."

She was quiet in the car and Mikey was more than happy not to listen to her. Usually, she'd be bending his ear about whatever the rant of the day was.

Instead she took the time to think about her relationship with Sonny. There was no doubt she took him for granted, but that was mutual. She thought it was true she knew more about him than he about her but that she reasoned was because she was older than him by five years. It would feel strange to discuss her love life with him. Well now she was gonna have to. She's somehow found herself in a position where she'll be forced to trade personal secrets to win back his confidence.

She also thought about his being disappointed in her. It was true. It explained the change of tone, the way he'd spoken to her in his garden. But their relationship was more equal than he thought. She knew this because it hurt to know he felt this way. She was as much dependent on his approval as he was on her – her *what*? Guidance? Example? Whatever it was, she wasn't giving it to him right now.

She didn't think of him as a son really, more like a best friend, different than with Shelley or Trevor or even her favourite cousin Michael. The main thing between them was trust – the very thing she'd let him down on. It was also their shared core beliefs, the way some things were just agreed, went without saying, like looking after the employees. She never had to convince him of the benefits of their approach, they shared those values. If either said someone had to be sacked, they'd go. It was so rare that they wouldn't question each other. Trust.

Some would say that it was none of his business who she had sex with, but Sita had been right. Dani's behaviour did have to match her morals, their morals, like it used to. She had to find Susanna and sort it out once and for all. She'd always thought their relationship would only end once she'd been sentenced for doing something to one of her girlfriends out of jealousy. This was getting more likely as time passed. She thought how it would be, visited in prison by Sonny. That would certainly put paid to what was left of his respect for her.

She'd originally planned to take Mikey in with her to meet the anxious Mr. Simpson, concerned about his son's behaviour. Now she decided to speak to him alone. She knew what she'd say because she's said it many times. Persuading young men his age to give up crime and go with a nine-to-five was now for her an art form. Success rates were alarmingly low but she loved a challenge, besides, she believed in what she said. The trickiest aspect was to gauge how much of her past to disclose in order to get them listening in the first place. Another bit of her personal life being used as currency.

Unfortunately though, without it she came across like another parent. Mr. Simpson senior would be there so it was an even more delicate balancing act.

"I used to be a villain, but I'm a nice girl now …"

There was no single incident that signaled the end of her career as a criminal. Rather it was a growing understanding of how the game would play out, the knowledge that sooner or later she was going to prison. That all she stole would somehow either get back in circulation having been stolen from her, or seized along with stuff she hadn't thieved. That the police didn't mind her getting away thirty times if they won the thirty-first round. And as she signed for her bail, they'd already be forgetting her and moving on to the next prisoner. It wasn't as personal as she'd like to think. She was no mastermind they lay in their beds fretting and planning how to finally snare. Just another kid prepared to take the high stakes gamble. That was the truth.

She'd mainly stolen cars as part of a gang that sold them on, in the days when the buyer could just say he bought it "in good faith" in order for the case file to end up in the bin. She didn't do it for the money and she didn't come from a disadvantaged background. It was always difficult to find a single answer.

She liked being part of that world. She liked being the only girl that wasn't dropped home or left indoors when things started to get interesting. She liked it that they knew she lived with a girlfriend and a baby. They didn't care. She'd always found it easier to be accepted in those circles. Everyone had his or her own label anyway. This one always sad, that one always sleeping on everyone else's sofa ...

When she was fifteen she'd thought it would be cool for people to know she'd been to prison. She wanted to be like one of those guys that never smiled. Those guys always seemed like real men to her. Not the grinning idiots who shouted and leered at the nice looking women in the street. Who could respect them?

But as she got older and friend after friend, acquaintance after acquaintance, went in and came out of prison, she saw the reality of the experience, the consequences. One by one she watched the dignity drain out of them, the respect of others turning to pity and impatience. The older she got the less she liked the idea of being an inmate.

She left Bristol with assurances from Mr. Simpson that he would allow her to speak to his son again. He made it clear that in his opinion, it was not his son's decision as to whether he would work for them. She let him talk. She knew a lot more about his son than he did.

She'd been pointed in Curtis Simpson's direction by a former employee who knew his older sister. The trouble he was getting into was unremarkable, but Dani was interested in his talent. He had the potential to be a very good mechanic. And Dani loved talent, no matter what it was. She wanted Curtis to work on the Village trucks while attending college. It would suit both parties if she could just get the overbearing dad onside.

Her mind turned back to Marie, as they sped back towards London. This was not going to be pleasant. Susanna might be jealous, but Marie had a nasty temper. Dani was no fan of jealousy, but as she suffered from it herself, particularly when it came to Susanna, she could understand it. It made sense even when it pissed her off. Marie on the other hand had a spiteful streak that went with the major weapon in her arsenal – Jess.

She gets the call just as they pass Newbury. It's lucky she has Mikey on board by the sounds of it. This is an urgent, short notice Meet. Trevor's already been called, as has Whisky, Tony and John, who's coming along as a favour. (Trevor has agreed to provide soldiers for when they drop off the drugs they owe Jason.)

Sonny's arranged for five cars to be plotted up around the area. The Meet will take place in Camden. Dani feels happier about the location. She's familiar with the area. She tells Mikey to drive straight there. They can get a coffee nearby and watch the arrivals from the rooftop terrace of a kebab shop belonging to a friend of Trevor's. It takes another hour to get there. By then she's amped, psyched up. Today is not about schoolboys fighting over skirt.

The Reckless Boys, a relatively young outfit, are in dispute with a couple of Turkish guys that are far too old to make up names for themselves. The Turks believe these boys are responsible for hijacking one of their lorries containing a large amount of stolen electrical goods.

The Reckless Boys are beginning to get a reputation for themselves. They're trying hard to live up to their stupid name. If they're responsible for this job, then this really is a worrying development, as the driver was threatened with a gun. That means both sides will be armed. An empty office will be used today. Dave, the organiser, has a brother who's an estate agent. They'll all be searched before entering the room, meaning the surrounding streets will be teeming with armed men and worse still, armed young boys.

Most of the soldiers will also be in the surrounding streets. She doesn't like too many in the room when she's dealing with young people. It only takes a second for them to get rowdy in a crowd. She'll be inside with Trevor, Mikey, John and, of course, Sonny. Ayrton and Paul from the Turks will come in along with two of the Reckless: Marvin and Colin.

Ayrton she's met once. Trevor had done business with him in the past. He's in his early thirties, about five ten, solid build and not about to take any shit from teenagers. Paul (who's actually Irish) has been his sidekick for a few years. She's told this by Trevor, who arrives shortly after she sits down by the railings with her juice.

"Ayrton's the placid one." He says this with an ironic raise of the eyebrow. "I heard he met Paul when he was doing a five stretch for supplying to undercover officers. Paul makes his money from hijacking lorries. He started buying gear from Ayrton with the proceeds and then they decided to team up.

Paul's useful in a row so Ayrton brings him to buy gear. You know how it is, class A gear needs class A protection."

Dani tells him what she knows of the other two. Marvin had at one time worked for her, about a year earlier. He'd shown promise working with his hands and been set up on a carpentry course. But he failed to attend either the course or work despite her efforts and in the end she'd let him go. She'd been sorry about it and always hoped he'd find a way to return. Colin she'd heard about. He was quickly making a name for himself and had a reputation for fearlessness. He needs to use his brain today.

Sonny arrives soon after Trevor. She watches him carefully as he walks towards her. Now they have to park all the other stuff and concentrate on not witnessing the start of a war only one side can win. He sits next to her, slapping her arm with the back of his hand.

"Thought I'd be picking you up from casualty."

She feels grateful for the nod then suddenly remembers she's promised to meet Marie.

"Shit! Marie!" She jumps up and walks to the other side of the roof.

Marie answers on the second ring. This alone makes her feel bad. She looks at her watch. Half past six.

"Marie, I'm really sorry, but something's come up."

"Don't worry about it."

"No, no, I really wanna see you. It's work."

"Work." Again the attitude, the tone, making it clear she has her own opinions about what Dani calls work.

"Look, I'll call you later. OK?"

"I don't know where I'll be."

Trevor is signalling impatiently to her.

"I gotta go. I'll call you tonight."

Marie hangs up. Fuck. Yet Dani's mind switches easily to Meet mode as she walks back over to them.

"Saddle up!" Trevor has his game face on.

Sonny checks his phone. "Yeah, let's go."

Dani takes a deep breath, glugs the last of her juice, looks at Sonny and nods. She really wants to talk to him now. She wishes she had the time. He nods back to reassure her. Knowing Sweets, Dani's probably already had a right going over. He can wait.

They file down the back stairs and pile into Mikey's car, along with John who's arrived on a motorcycle. Tony and Whisky are round the corner in a car with Simon and Abdi. The venue's just around the block so they pull up almost immediately. Ayrton and Paul step out of a Range Rover. Dani is sitting at the back of Mikey's car in the middle and deliberately gets out last. The youngsters are late. Not a good start.

A car suddenly speeds into the yard at the back of the building, with Colin driving. He and Marvin get out of the obviously hired convertible GTi. They're dripping in diamond chains, bracelets, watches, designer clothes, the whole shebang. Dani sighs. It's gonna be hard to get any sense out of these boys. She wishes she'd worn her suit.

She walks into the room and sits down at the table, set up with bottles of water. She double checks the bottles and cups are all made from plastic. Then she checks there are no glass ashtrays in sight. She already has a bad feeling in the pit of her stomach, which only gets worse when Colin and Marvin bounce unconcerned into the office. Ayrton and Paul shake her hand before greeting the others. Marvin throws himself down sullenly into one of the chairs. Colin sits next to him, straightening the chains around his neck as he takes in his surroundings curiously. If anything he seems distracted. He actually looks at his gaudy watch. Trevor raises an eyebrow.

"Yeah, watchas. I'm on some next ting yeah, so tell me what I'm doing here cos I got things going on." This was Marvin.

Sonny is already sending messages on his phone.

Dani glances quickly over at Ayrton. If he's angry, he's not showing it. In fact he looks amused. Paul on the other hand is staring unblinkingly at Colin.

Trevor speaks first. They do this sometimes with younger boys. Fear usually concentrates their minds.

"You steal these guys' stuff?"

Dani can see he's not warming to these boys.

"What fucking stuff!" Again Marvin. He says this as though he's bored.

Dani looks at Colin, who is fingering the links on his gold bracelet. It must be new. She already knows they've stolen the goods. It's obvious to her. It would be obvious to a blind man. Neither Ayrton nor Paul are speaking so Trevor continues, "Cos if you have, you owe them and you're gonna pay. Understand?"

Colin finally speaks up, looking Trevor squarely in the eyes.

"This don't seem very neutral to me. Anyway, you can't prove nuffin."

Dani closes her eyes. Fucking idiot. That must be the world record, for speed of admitting a crime.

She's about to start talking before things get nasty, when she glances at Paul. This time he's staring intently at Marvin.

She looks at Ayrton, sitting back in his chair, a content look on his face. Maybe they think she's just going to talk the goods straight out of these boys' hands. They seem very confident. It's not as if they've ever seen her in action before. Then, too late, she realises the only purpose of this Meet is to give crazy Paul over there a good look at these boys, who he's going to hunt down after the Meet's over. She knows Marvin has no idea how bad this can get. She starts talking, fast.

"Come on Marvin, you know this is neutral, OK. I'm looking for everyone to leave here as soon as, but these geezers ain't gonna go without their stuff or some decent cash. Listen, if you made a mistake, didn't know the lorry was belonging to them then fair enough." She spreads her hands appeasingly. "All we have to do is sort out a timescale for getting the stuff back to them or paying them back. Everyone makes mistakes in this game. It don't have to be no long argument. We just sort it out and you move on. OK?"

Colin chuckles.

"I dunno what you lot are on about. We never took nothing."

Dani clenches her jaw until her temples begin to pulse. What is it with these young geezers? Why can they never see the danger that's right in front of them? She turns on him angrily.

"How are you making your money, Colin?"

"I'm making moves innit." He says this with pride.

"What moves?"

"None of your fucking business and I never lifted them TVs, OK."

"Who said they was TVs?" This from Paul.

Colin doesn't miss a beat.

"You did."

Paul stands up.

"We're done here."

"Wait a sec Paul."

Dani is certain now the Turks don't want to make a deal, now they know who to hurt. Paul walks around the table to stand directly over Colin.

"Everyone in this room knows you've had that stuff, OK son. I'm gonna get paid one way or another, either today or tomorrow, it's up to you."

Colin shifts in his seat but only to allow himself to meet Paul's gaze. Marvin is looking over at Dani. Paul is not pretty, close up.

Paul nods to Ayrton.

"Why don't you sort the bits and pieces outside?" He's talking about paying Dani, Trevor and Sonny off. "I'll take it from here."

"No, hold on." Things are moving too fast for Dani's liking. "Let me talk to them."

"There's really no need. I have it all sorted." Paul smiles agreeably.

Dani tries to keep the anxiety out of her voice.

"Just give me a little time, Paul OK?"

Again he smiles.

"Fine."

He and Ayrton go outside to make calls. Dani approaches Colin, ignoring Marvin for the moment. She knows Colin is the one she needs to convince.

"See him?" She's pointing towards Trevor. "He doesn't like you, but he's not gonna waste his time thinking about you. Minute he walks out of here he'll forget you. Those guys, on the other hand, have spent the last ten minutes memorising your face. Not him." She indicates Marvin.

"Just you, Colin."

"Why me?"

He hasn't panicked; she'll give him that.

"Because you act like you're the main guy."

He nods. She's beginning to wonder if this boy is not quite right. He doesn't seem to have any emotional responses. It makes him difficult to read.

"So?" he says flatly.

"So, you looking for a war?"

"They got fat pockets. They ain't got time to be running around after kids like us."

Unbelievable. Now she's getting pissed off. She glances at Marvin.

"What you got to say about this?"

He shrugs.

"We never took their stuff."

"You're lying and even if you aren't, you're the ones that's gonna pay."

"But they don't need that money!"

Sonny has said nothing throughout. He is clearly getting riled though; she can tell because he's furiously punching his phone, sending messages constantly. He looks up.

"You got a problem."

Colin looks over at him. Sonny says,

"How many boys you bring with you?"

"None. Just us."

Sonny knows they're lying. "You're one down."

Dani looks skyward. "Do you even know what you're doing? You better start thinking about how you're gonna get him back."

Marvin is properly worried now.

"Who have they got?"

He's right out of his depth while Colin seems to think shit happens.

Trevor gets up now. He's had enough.

"We're talking about twenty Gees. You gonna pay it or what?"

"How much?" says Marvin.

"No." Colin's tone is firm, neither angry nor defensive.

"Fine, fuck off then." Trevor looks at Dani. "We're not here to wipe anyone's fucking noses. Your little friend will be in casualty by tomorrow and you can all go into hiding together."

Dani is looking at Marvin, as he stands up, urged on by Colin. They're actually going to leave …

"Wait. Marvin you sure you don't wanna just let off one of them chains you're wearing? Could save you a massive headache." Not to mention your limbs, she's thinking.

Colin steps up to Dani in an almost confrontational way, yet he speaks mildly.

"You look after your soldiers and I'll look after mine. OK, sis?"

She blinks, taking a second to register his words.

"What did you say?"

"You heard me." He's impassive.

Trevor actually laughs. "Go on then, fuck off. Come on Dani, we're going."

Sonny, John and Mikey all get to their feet as Dani tries one last time,

"Marvin?"

Nothing. He must be afraid of Colin.

"Like I said," says Colin, moving to block her view of his sidekick, "you look after your soldiers and I'll look after mine."

He turns and leaves, followed by a nervous Marvin. Trevor has to nudge her out of the shock.

"Forget it. Come on."

They walk out towards Paul's Range Rover.

"Get in the car, Dani."

Trevor obviously wants to prevent her saying anything to them about Marvin. He can see she's having trouble letting go. She climbs in poker-faced. He returns to the car minutes later, with a wad of money.

"They wouldn't let us refuse it."

Dani nods her head. This wasn't a freebie. Them Turks got what they came for. There's no point in arguing. They'd given those boys a chance.

They count the money and leave.

8

Midnight Blue

M ikey drops John off at his bike first, Dani again
sitting in the middle at the back.
"Safe Johnny."
Johnny looks at her and laughs.
"Look after your soldiers."
"I know! Cheeky little bastard." She is shaking her head.

She wants to speak to Sonny, so they transfer to Trevor's
car. She's quiet as they make their way over to Charlie's.
Trevor turns in his seat to look at her at the traffic lights.

"They'll be alright. Probably just get a bit of a van job."

She nods. They probably deserve being lifted off the
street, driven round in a van having the shit kicked out of
them and being warned about their future conduct.

But what if they were stupid enough to retaliate? She
feels different this time. She'd done nothing to improve the
situation and in fact had probably made it worse for them. She
sighs. Trevor's right, though. There was nothing she could do.

She returns to her own situation. She doesn't have the

strength to deal with Marie today, so she sits down opposite Sonny in the back yard at Charlie's. They both roll their spliffs in silence.

She takes a deep drag and throws her head back, exhaling.

"OK, look Son …"

He looks down at the table, for her benefit rather than his own.

"You know I was with Susanna a long time ago. Even though we split up, we never did properly."

His brow furrows.

"We should have but we didn't."

"Why?"

She gulps. Then she glares.

"Ain't she got a drug problem, Dani?"

He's asking this tentatively but her temples pulse.

"She is a fucking person, you know! She's not just someone you talk about cos you're glad it ain't you!"

"I know but …"

"What did I tell you about that? Which one of us has got the fucking right to say someone else is no good?"

Mentally he kicks himself for setting her off.

"I'm not saying that …"

"She's clean now, anyway. And even if she weren't, I'd still have the same problem." She lowers her voice, making eye contact. "You understand, Son?"

It's best if he says nothing. She swallows, leaning closer.

"Every time I'm with someone else, I'm hoping that person can make me forget her." She shakes her head sadly. "Marie can't."

"So – you gonna be with Susanna?"

She holds her hands up in resignation.

"I dunno. I got some stuff with her that needs sorting out."

She's pissed off at having to discuss it at all, but if she could only make him understand. She jabs at her chest.

"It's still her in there. She still does the same things that make me ... Forget it." She obviously doesn't want to think about it so he just watches, not wishing to wind her up any further. She sighs again.

"I know what I said about playing around and I know what a fucking hypocrite that makes me, but it ain't that simple with her."

"What's that supposed to mean?"

She can hear in his voice how disgusted he still is with her.

"Son, I do care what you think of me. I try to impress you as much as you try to impress me."

"Whasat?"

He looks at her, surprised. She smiles at his embarrassment.

"You gonna make me say it again? Look I mean it OK, but things with her, they're kinda upside down."

He looks at her again. She looks terrible. Tired, worried, worn out. He no longer feels like giving her a hard time.

"I ain't gonna tell you what you already know, but I think you should be careful about her, Dani."

"Believe me when I tell you it's not her. It's me."

"You can't let the boys see you doing them things."

"I know, I know."

"You gotta sort it out with Marie."

"Yeah. I'm gonna, soon as." She wonders when or if she'll see Jess again. "Fuck it. Let's play pool."

They get up and walk over to an upbeat Trevor.

"I'm taking the wife out tonight, why don't you call Sweets

and Marie and see if they're up for it?"

"Nah," says Sonny.

"Come on, we'll make a night of it after all that bollocks today. We've got a sitter and everything. Just bring your lot round, plenty of room."

He's not joking. His house is huge. Dani smiles.

"Yeah, why not."

She sees the way Sonny looks at her. He doesn't want her to tell even Trevor. Fine. Right now he can have whatever he wants.

"Marie's got evening class but call Sweets, go on. I'm gonna need to change though."

Two hours later, after much to-ing and fro-ing with children, cars and partners, they are in a Thai restaurant in Chelsea. Trevor, Paula, Sonny, Sita, Mikey, Derek and Dani are crowded around a table. Trevor takes centre stage. It's not easy for Dani to take time off from trying to find Susanna, but their high spirits help. Despite Mikey and Trevor's best efforts, she is refusing to drink any alcohol. Both she and Derek are driving. They all agree to go on to a gay club in central London. Dani, Sonny and Sita travel in her car.

"So I take it you two have made up then?"

"For now," says Sonny. "She's a bit too stressed out for me to nag her anymore."

"Piss off." Dani is smiling, unable to hide how relieved she is.

They all arrive at the club in good spirits. It's spread over three floors and they go to the top floor because they can see everything from there. They're in off duty mode.

Dani and Sonny are inseparable for most of the night.

Trevor is determined to lift their spirits. He knew they were both concerned about Marvin but he was more pragmatic about it. No one could be helped if they didn't want it.

He's playing the fool on the dance floor with Derek and Mikey, while the rest watch, laughing. Paula is ignoring him, she's used to his performances. She hasn't seen Dani for a couple of weeks.

"How's Marie?"

Dani doesn't want to lie to her.

"I ain't really gonna be seeing much of her anymore, to be honest."

"Oh, I'm sorry."

"No it's cool. Just ain't working out, that's all."

"What about Jess? Will you still see her?"

"Aah, that's not really looking so good."

Paula smiles at her sympathetically.

"You can borrow some of mine. I've got loads."

Dani laughs.

"Thanks. How are those babies anyway?"

"Like their dad," Paula says, indicating Trevor who's doing what can only be described as the funky chicken – to funky house.

Later on, Dani is leaning over the railings watching the dancers below. She sees Sita approaching from the side. She looks around, "Where's Sonny?"

"Gone to the bar. He's fine."

"Are we cool, Sweets?"

"Course we are, Dani. I wasn't trying to put you down."

"Yeah, I know. You were just being honest." She grins. "I hate that about you."

Sita grins back and puts a hand on her back.

"Are you OK?"

"Yeah. You can't go nowhere with this lot and be miserable"

"That's true …"

Dani doesn't hear the rest of what's said because she's spotted who she thinks could be Susanna's friend Sophie, down on the lower floor. She feels her whole body go hot. She's glad she's only been smoking.

She waits until Sweets stops talking.

"Tell Sonny I've just gone for a wander." He would want to know.

"Shall I come with you?"

"No. I'm just gonna have a look." She winks, hoping Sweets will think she's on the prowl. It works.

"Don't pick up any strays."

"Just looking. See ya in a mo."

She walks along by the railing, looking down again at the lower floor. Sophie has two drinks in her hand. She moves out of sight and returns empty-handed to the bar. She's handed two further drinks from someone at the bar whose face Dani can't see. The girl at the bar looks oddly familiar, but Dani pays no further attention, that's not who she's looking for.

She moves quickly down the stairs, greeting a couple of soldiers and pointing them up to where the others are as she goes, keeping to the corners on the lower floor until – she sees her.

She's standing in a dark corner by herself, seemingly hiding, looking nervously about her. Sophie's talking to someone a couple of feet away.

Dani moves until she's directly opposite and then begins walking towards her as Susanna's sixth sense draws her gaze in Dani's direction. She stalls for a moment, taking in Dani's trousers, her favourite midnight blue shirt; the one Susanna had bought for her. Dani's watching, still moving towards her. She's usually bad at reading Susanna but she catches that look before she sees her expression change to worry, then fear.

Susanna looks quickly to her left and then back at Dani who's now standing in front of her. She holds up her hands defensively, looking quickly again towards the bar,

"Dani, my girlfriend's here."

Dani steps in closer, as if she hasn't heard. She smiles.

"Where the fuck have you been?" She slips her arm around Susanna's waist, stroking her back.

"Please, don't. She's gonna see you."

She puts her lips to Susanna's ear, slipping the other arm around her waist. Susanna's hands hover near Dani's arms. She knows it will only make things worse to try and push her away like that.

"You gonna let me fuck you tonight, Suse?"

"Stop it. Please. Look Dani, I'll meet you tomorrow, OK? I promise. Just stop!"

Dani is kissing her cheek, her ear, her neck.

"We're meeting now."

Just then, Sophie looks over, her eyes wide with shock. She wheels around, hoping to distract Susanna's girlfriend or head her off, but it's too late.

Carly stands transfixed, watching Dani's hands moving over her girlfriend's body.

She looks at Susanna's face, trying to understand the expression. She looks upset, yet she's not pushing Dani away. She can see her giving in. Their eyes meet before Susanna looks down into Dani's chest, her hands clenched on her forearms.

"Are you happy now? She's watching. Everyone's fucking watching!"

Dani hasn't even bothered to look over and see who the girlfriend is.

"Shall I tell you why she's over there and not here?"

"Not exactly a fair fight with all your soldiers is it?" Susanna says bitterly.

Dani smirks.

"You see any soldiers here?"

Finally Susanna tries to push her away, but Dani is about to turn her head in Carly's direction.

"No!" Susanna puts one hand on Dani's cheek. She doesn't want her to know who it is. Dani smiles.

"The reason she's over there is because when she sees me with you, she knows."

Susanna looks at her with hatred as both hands drop to her sides.

"What does she know, Dani?"

"That you're mine."

She says this as though it's such a simple fact only dense people wouldn't know it. She kisses her on the lips.

"Stop it." They can both hear the defeat in Susanna's voice.

"Come on." Dani takes her hand. "You ready?" She's no longer smiling.

They walk towards the stairs hand in hand. Susanna looks at the floor as she's led up towards the exit. Upstairs on the top floor, Sonny watches as they leave.

Down below, a bewildered Carly slumps against the bar, mouth hanging grotesquely agape, Susanna's drink still in her hand. Then rage starts to take hold as Carly comes to her senses. She looks around the club at friends who can't meet her eyes. She looks at the floors above. If Dani was here alone she's going after them. She sees Trevor watching her from the top floor. Sonny's also glaring down at her. She turns away as anger and shame burn her cheeks lava red. She grabs at the retreating Sophie's arm.

"You tell your fucking slag friend that I better not see her by herself!"

Sophie pulls away angrily.

"Let go of me! I told you before, I don't want anything to do with it."

She storms off out of the club with her friend Helen, to look for a cab. Not this again!

Dani and Susanna walk up the stairs to street level and towards Dani's car, parked opposite. They cross the road and run into John and three or four others.

Dani is distracted.

"You alright, John?" She keeps walking.

"I need to talk to you, Dani."

"I'm leaving right now," she says indicating Susanna with her eyes, "but Sonny and them lot are on the top floor."

"No. It's you I need to see."

She's getting irritated. She stops.

"Can't it wait?"

"Not really."

She notices he keeps glancing at Susanna. She doesn't like people looking at her at the best of times. She looks pointedly at John now, following his gaze to Susanna and back.

"Fuck you looking at?"

Now John looks directly at Susanna. "Are you alright?"

She avoids his eyes as Dani snaps, "Don't fucking talk to her. What do you … aaaah, yeah!"

She nods, smiling nastily, her mind's eye returning to the girl at the bar.

"What's your sister's name again, John?"

"Dani, can we just go?" Susanna snatches her hand away from Dani's, folding her arms across her chest. "Unlock the car please?"

Dani, the keys already in her hand, presses the button. The click of the doors unlocking is audible. Her eyes remain on John as she walks forward, opening the car door for Susanna, who gets in the passenger seat, staring straight ahead, her jaw working.

Dani sneers at John.

"You think you know her?"

She slams the car door shut, taking a moment to look carefully at each of the boys with him, one after the other. One boy turns his head away. He has no desire to be involved in any dispute with someone who can call on Trevor as backative.

She gets in the car, shaking her head, and drives off wordlessly.

Susanna glances over at her.

"I'm not going to bed with you tonight, so if that's what you're thinking you can just fucking drop me home."

Dani doesn't answer. Nothing else is said by either of them for the entire journey to Dani's place. This time Susanna walks directly into the kitchen and sits at the table. Caught off guard, Dani follows her.

"I'm sorry."

"No you're not, Dani." She's still pissed off.

Deep breath. "I am, Suse. I just needed to be with you."

"Really? For how long?"

"What?"

"How long do you need me for this time?"

She folds her arms and looks directly at Dani, who's confused.

"What are you talking about?"

"I'm talking about you wanting me when you feel like it."

"What do you mean, when I feel like it? I can't fucking find you half the time, and when I do, you disappear in the middle of the fucking night!"

"Once. I did that once."

"Susanna, what the fuck are you on about?" Dani was about to sit, but she remains standing as Susanna says grimly, "Do you wanna know why I left?"

"Maybe you missed your little girlfriend?" Dani's sarcastic now.

"Maybe I'm tired of hearing all your empty promises!"

"My what?"

"Your empty promises, I said Dani! 'We're gonna do this Suse, we're gonna do that Suse …' When? When is it going to happen?"

Dani's brow descends as her anger rises.

"I've spent the last twelve years waiting for you to let me know." She's shouting now.

"Let you know what?" Susanna's voice is loud too.

"When you're ready."

"When I'm ready? When I'm ready?" Her voice gets even louder. "No, Dani. I've always been here, always available to you. You convinced me the obstacle was me but it's you. It's been you all along."

"Suse …"

"No, Dani! You tell me why we aren't together."

"Because you …"

"Because *me* nothing Dani, it's because of you!" She's hot, yelling now. "Am I some sort of fucking whore?"

Dani's eyes are wide with shock. She can say nothing.

"Dani. You can walk into a club, walk up to me in front of my girlfriend! Do you understand? That is my fucking girlfriend! And the whole fucking club! And kiss me, feel me up, drag me out and take me home. You can do all that, yet you can't be with me, mmmh? How is that? You tell me cos I wanna hear!" She's on her feet now, pointing. "Nothing? OK, I'll tell you shall I? Two possible explanations: number one, I'm a whore. But then, I don't let anyone else do this to me so it must be the second one. Do you wanna know what the second one is? You Dani, are a fucking coward! You don't want to be with me because I know the real Dani. Not the good Dani that all your little lost soldiers march behind. No, I know the other Dani. Don't I? DON'T I? And you can't handle that so you keep me hanging. And you make sure you fuck up every relationship I have!"

She is screaming now. Dani finds her voice.

"What?! We both do that. No Susanna, we both do that. Look at the state of my fucking back!"

"Yes you're right, Dani, I didn't want you to tell me you love me one night and then fuck Marie the next. OK!"

Suddenly, Dani's anger evaporates. She holds her head. She's getting tired of people calling out her weaknesses, telling her who she is and who she isn't.

"Do you love her?" Susanna's question sounds more like an accusation.

"Marie? No."

"Does she make you forget me?"

"No." She says this quietly.

"Well, *I've* found someone that can help me forget you!"

Dani's look of shock changes to something akin to malice. She moves around the table, backing Susanna up against the wall.

"You fucking say that to me." She grinds her teeth, shaking. "I'll have her in the back of a van by tomorrow."

"I don't care. I'm not afraid of you, and I'm not doing this with you anymore, Dani."

"I'll do her and her fucking brother."

"Stop it."

Dani's panting.

"I swear I'll break every fucking bone in her body. I'll leave her in the fucking woods, Suse. She won't ..."

"STOP!" She pushes at her shoulders. "That's all you fucking do, Dani. Drive everyone else away from me and then leave me alone."

"I what? I wish I could fucking drive everyone away. Just once I'd like you to turn up and say 'I'm not with anybody, Dani.' Just fucking once! Why don't you try it?"

"Why? So you can lock me away for good?"

"You fucking spent the whole of the other night telling me how much you miss me, how much you're so in love with me ..." She's mocking Susanna's voice.

"Get out of my way. I want to go."

"Oh you wanna go now? What happened to all that love, Suse? Did it die?"

"Yes. I fucking hate you!"

Dani's lip curls.

"Will you hate me when I climb in your girlfriend's window, Suse?"

"Get away from me."

"I'll find out where she lives."

Susanna closes her eyes as Dani spits, "You see when I

find her, I'm gonna ask who was born first, her or John. That way I'll know who to send first."

Susanna juts out her chin. "It won't stop me hating you."

Dani draws back suddenly, reaching for a glass on the counter. She turns and hurls it against the wall. Susanna flinches as it shatters, but she remains standing. Dani snatches up a bottle. It too shatters against the wall.

"You fucking hate me?" She's panting again. "Go then." She kicks the nearest chair across the floor and strides out of the kitchen.

Susanna stands in the same place, breathing heavily, chewing at the inside of her cheek. Dani is in the bedroom, roughly pulling on her black tracksuit. She shoves her feet down hard into trainers. She takes her flick knife from the cupboard, slamming the door shut.

Susanna's hand goes to her head. Broken glass crunches under her shoes as she walks from the kitchen. They meet in the hallway.

"No! Dani, stop." She knows exactly what it means when Dani dresses in black. She moves in front of her. "Just stop."

"She ain't having you."

Dani walks around her. Susanna loses it again.

"Why can't you fucking fight for me instead of fighting other people?"

"Cos fighting everyone else is easier." She opens the door.

"But Dani if you go out there, I'll still be here."

"What am I gonna fight for you for? You hate me."

Susanna sighs. "And yet I'm still here."

Dani waits. She closes the door.

"What is it you want from me?" She's worn out now, drained.

"You don't know? You don't know what happens when we sleep together, Dani? When we sleep?"

She's still too weary to speak as Susanna continues, softly. "You put your whole weight on top of me."

Dani turns, watching her.

"You put your arm over my chest and hold my arm. You put your leg over mine, your head on my shoulder. I don't think you do that with anyone else because they couldn't stand it."

Dani knows it's true.

"You hold me down so I can't get away. You do that in your sleep! The first time you did that I felt safe, so loved. Like you needed me. Like you would never let me go. And then we went to the café in the morning and you told me we would be together, we would have our babies. And then you let me go."

"But you've got your …"

"So what? I have an addiction. I love all of you, why can't you love all of me … like you say you do?"

"I do."

"No, you don't. And now I'm clean and you're still talking to me about the future. Dani, I don't have a future with you."

"Why are you saying that to me?"

"Before, when you used to do that to me, I'd go on a bender."

Dani's shaking her head.

"But your therapy guy said you had to be away from me to get clean."

"So fucking what, Dani? That's what I mean. When you want me, you don't care what anyone says, so why aren't we together?"

Dani is silent for a long time. Susanna sighs. There's no point in prolonging this. She moves towards the door. Dani blocks her path.

"Wait! Wait!" She holds her hands up. "No. Look I'm sorry. Just … just …" She's numb but she won't let her leave under any circumstances. She has no idea how she, *they* came to be in this position. "I want you with me."

Susanna shakes her head, "No, you don't."

"Suse, you know I love you."

"I know."

"Then what are you saying? You don't love me?"

"No."

"Oh yeah, I get it now. You're gonna use that fucking crash test dummy to see what it's like when you hit the wall." Dani's getting angry again, she still can't understand how this has happened.

"You know what?" she says. "You're right, Suse. I can't always trust myself when I'm with you. But that doesn't mean I don't want to be with you, OK?"

"Who are you trying to convince?"

"I never want you to go."

"Then why don't you stop me? Like you are now?"

"You have no idea what happens when you go, what I've been doing since the last time I saw you. Suse, I'm not with you because I don't want to put any more pressure on you than I already do. I know what I do to you. I'm not blind!"

Susanna is finally looking at her again.

"Suse, there is no way I'm letting you leave me today. Whatever I did before, I'm stopping you now. I don't know if you're right about why we're not together but I don't fucking care. Maybe I was scared or selfish or whatever you want to say, but me and you? There's no way we are gonna end today!"

Dani takes Susanna's hands, lowering her voice. "Come and sit down, please. I'm sorry. I'm really sorry. I'd never dream that of all things you'd be upset with me about was you'd think I don't want you. Suse, you climb out another woman's bed to come see me! I never turn you away. Do you think that could happen with anyone else? It goes both ways. We can both get crazy! I never refuse you and I hate it when you go. I hate being without you. You must know that. I don't even know how you had the guts to stand there and tell me you've found someone else, but I'm not even wasting my time on that. I already know that's not true."

"How? How do you know that?" Susanna allows herself to be pulled back down the hallway.

"Because I *would* know. It's just the same with me and you. You can't lie about that."

She is stroking her hands as Susanna lowers her head.

"Sometimes I want to hurt you."

"I know, but you're still in love with me, Suse. I'm ready to be with you now. Right now. I meant everything I said." She kisses her.

Susanna doesn't resist.

"I don't want anything to happen to Carly."

"It won't Suse. I promise."

"It's not right, what we did to her."

"I know, I know. I'm sorry." They're kissing each other now.

"Dani, I don't care about the you everyone says you are. The you you're trying to be. I want you to be yourself. A good person."

Dani's not sure this is true. "It's just … you never set any limits, Suse. "

"But that's not for me to do. I don't want you to change."

"Yeah, but sometimes I think you'd forgive anything I do."

"Maybe I would. I love you. It's up to you to control yourself."

"I know. But – what if it's you that brings out the worst in me?"

"What if I'm the only one who sees the best in you, Dani?"

"Maybe I would be better if we stayed together."

Susanna has a sharp intake of breath.

"Are we really gonna do this?"

"Well, you know I'm not gonna let you go, Suse."

They stand holding each other now.

"Shall we go and get your things tomorrow?"

Susanna draws back to look at her.

"Dani, we don't have to rush."

"It's not that. Look, whatever you want, I want you here. But it's up to you, OK?"

Susanna smiles, tilting her head to the side.

"Are you tired?"

Dani nods, grinning.

"Liar. Take me to bed?"

Dani is already reaching around her back to undo her dress …

In bed they're whispering.

"I don't want no one else touching you."

"I don't want you sleeping with Marie anymore."

"Spread your legs."

"No."

"Want me to hold you down?"

"Fuck off."

"You're all mine now, remember."

Susanna is giggling as she climbs on top.

"It goes both ways, babe."

Dani wakes to find Susanna asleep, her head resting on Dani's thigh. Her leg is numb, but she doesn't care. She runs her fingers through Susanna's hair, stroking her cheek.

"Suse?"

"Hmmm?"

"Come here."

Susanna crawls up between her legs, resting on her chest. She's barely awake. Dani kisses her forehead.

"Wake up."

"What time is it?"

"3-ish."

"Dani! I've got work tomorrow."

"I don't think so," she says, her hands moving down to Susanna's breasts. She rolls her over onto her back, moving down to kiss her.

"Stop."

"You love me?"

"Yes, but I also love sleep."

Dani climbs on top as they kiss. She stops, looking down at her.

"Do you love her?"

The smile leaves Susanna's face.

"Get off me."

"No, it's OK. I'm not gonna get angry."

"Get off please."

Dani sighs as she rolls off.

"Is that why you woke me up?" Susanna's heating up again.

It is – but, "No," Dani lies. "Are you gonna answer me, though?"

"Do you love Marie?" counters Susanna.

"I already told you."

"What about the baby?" She doesn't know Jessica's name because she doesn't want to.

"Yes," admits Dani, "but not enough to lose you."

"Ditto."

Dani gets up. Susanna follows her into the living room.

"I thought you weren't gonna get angry."

"Why don't you try it then?"

"This is stupid, Dani. Be careful, there's glass on the floor."

"You were gonna have a baby with *her*."

"I want to have my baby with you, dummy! I was just trying to get you to commit to me, OK? Now, can we stop this?"

"Do you love her?"

"Oh boy! Look I'm not going to say I don't care for her, but I still left with you. She was kind to me. She tried to help me. She even forgave me after she knew I'd been with you, but I still choose you every time, don't I? Now, I'm asking you nicely to drop it."

Dani chews her lower lip, considering her options. What she really wants to do is find Carly and give her a little warning, make sure she stays away. But she's already promised nothing's gonna happen.

She takes Susanna's hand and leads her back to the bedroom …

9

Oh-ohh

Susanna wakes to banging at the front door. Dani is disoriented and tired. It takes a while to wake her. She is lying across Susanna, who is whispering urgently into her ear.

"Dani, someone's at the door."

Dani raises her head and looks down at her. She smiles. My Suse. This will be just as good as last night. This is the part when Susanna is the most gentle, the most relaxed. Vulnerable. She will lie comfortably, stroking and kissing while Dani just stares. She can handle it. She will tell Dani she loves her, Dani will say: "more." She will laugh and repeat it over and over, until they end up making love again. Dani's hand slides down to her hip. Then she hears it.

"Open the fucking door!"

The memories of the previous night flood back as she jumps out of the bed.

"Look at the wall, Suse."

Susanna unthinkingly does as she is asked, while Dani retrieves something from inside a cupboard.

"Stay here."

She leaves the room, closing the door firmly behind her. Susanna sits up quickly, searching for her clothes. She hopes Carly isn't stupid enough to come here.

Dani has thrown on her track bottoms and a T-shirt. She puts on trainers then goes to the door and listens.

"Come on. Open the fucking door!"

"They might not be here," someone says.

"Lets find out then shall we?" the first male voice grates.

There is kicking at the door, the sound of a foot landing next to the lock.

"Trevor?"

"Yeah! Open the fucking door!"

For a second she's relieved but then the tone of his voice registers. She puts the weapon in the key cupboard by the door before opening it. No sense in pressing anymore of his buttons. Sonny's there too. She looks from one to the other.

"Where's the fucking fire?"

"Have a nice time last night, didya?" Trevor is pissed off.

She doesn't want to answer, doesn't want him to know Susanna is there if it is not necessary.

"Yeah, it was alright." She's trying to catch Sonny's eye to get a clue.

"Still good is she?"

Shit.

"It's her again, innit?"

Dani clenches her jaw at Trevor.

"Look if this is about John and his fucking ugly sister, just tell me. I'll fucking sort it myself."

"Oh you will, will ya?"

She looks at Sonny. "What's going on?" Then abruptly back at Trevor. "Why you tryna kick my fucking door off?"

"Can we come in?"

She's seen Trevor barge into people's houses like this in the past. She's never been on the receiving end. She knows she has no choice, so she steps aside. What's bothering her even more is Sonny avoiding eye contact with her. Trevor marches straight into the living room, Sonny follows. He leaves the talking to Trevor.

"Sleeping is she?"

Not likely after your fucking racket. "Yeah."

"How d'ya find her?"

"What do you mean?"

"That's what you been doing all this time, innit? Looking for her. That's why you been busy anytime anyone calls you."

She says nothing.

"Go on. How did you find her?"

"She was in the club last night." She is not liking all this interest in Susanna.

"So you found her yourself?"

"I told you, she was in the club. Why's everyone so fucking interested in my love life all of a sudden?"

"So you didn't hire some youth" (he pronounces it yoot) "on the sly, tell him he's on the firm and send him looking for her."

Fuck! Dennis! Fuck! She's not stupid. She's not gonna try and talk her way out of this one. She looks at Sonny, who is now looking at her. It only takes a second for him to know it's true. She sinks down onto the nearest chair, her forehead sliding down into the palm of her hand.

Trevor's not done with her yet.

"Guess where your little private dick is now?"

He's shouting. She looks up quizzically.

"The Turks have got him!" This is the first time Sonny's spoken.

Dani hopes Susanna can't hear this and is almost afraid to ask. She says, "Why've they got him?"

Trevor's shouting again.

"He rides with Colin. If you'd fucking had a proper look at him before taking him on, you'd have known that. He was with them when they did the Turks' lorry."

Dani is crushed. She'd forgotten all about Dennis the minute she found Susanna. Trevor goes off again, not giving her a chance to take it all in.

"Apparently they're driving him into Epping, when he starts calling your name, talking about he's a soldier."

"Not before they broke his wrist though!"

Sonny looks at her, shaking his head. He stands up.

"We need to go and get him back, if he's ours."

Trevor's temple is pulsing.

"He's not fucking ours, is he? He's Dani's personal secret soldier, ain't he?" He looks down at the broken glass, following the trail to the kitchen. "So, what? She just gonna hide in the room?"

No answer.

"Why don't she come out?"

Dani is shaking her head.

"Not today."

Trevor jabs his finger down towards her face.

"Listen, don't start all this fucking shit with that fucking girl again, Dani. I ain't playing!"

She avoids both their gazes, rubbing the back of her neck. She needs sleep. She needs to get Susanna out of there. Needs to get Dennis back. Needs to speak to Sonny. Mostly, she needs a holiday from people exposing her every weakness and then stomping on her. She takes a deep breath.

"I'm gonna get dressed."

She turns to leave the room but Trevor's still not done. "And what about John?"

She turns back.

"Fuck John! I don't give a fuck about John or his fucking fool sister!" She is beginning to lose it.

"So what, then? You just gonna walk in caveman style and drag this girl out from under Carly whenever you need a dose?"

"Mind your own fucking business."

She resents the implication that Susanna and Carly are a couple. She leaves the room, glancing at Sonny as she goes. She's not pissed off with him. Letting him down is becoming a nasty habit.

In the bedroom, Susanna is on the phone whispering to Sophie. She's sitting on the side of the bed, fully dressed in a mixture of last night's clothes and things she's left here in the past in her own drawer. She hangs up as Dani enters. Dani says quietly, "You alright, Suse?"

"What's happened?" She could only make out a few words during all the shouting.

"Nothing. Just Trevor and Sonny is all." She changes into jeans. "But me and them are leaving in a minute, OK."

"Where're you going?"

"I'll phone you later, Suse."

She takes a pile of bank notes from a drawer.

"Where, Dani?"

"Don't come out until we leave." She grabs a jacket.

"Dani!" She whispers furiously.

"What's wrong?" Dani stops and turns to look at her.

"Are you going to tell me where you are going?"

"No."

Susanna sighs. Here we go again.

"Do I need to worry about you?"

"No."

"What time will you be back?"

"I'll call you as soon as I can. Please stay in here until we go."

Susanna watches as Dani takes green overalls out of the wardrobe and bundles them up under her arm.

"Don't come out till we're gone."

Dani doesn't kiss her before leaving the room. Susanna says nothing, watching as she closes the bedroom door firmly behind her.

She hears Dani call into the living room.

"Come on, let's go."

10

Looking Back

Trevor and Sonny are smoking in the car. Dani is too tired, hungry and paranoid to do the same but at least Trevor seems calmer as a result. Sonny turns to look at her.

"We're gonna have to say Dennis is new, we hadn't told Trev yet and we're gonna deal with him."

She looks at Trevor in the rearview mirror. He is silent. She considers apologising to him, but thinks it better to wait. He can feel her eyes.

"When did you sign him on?"

"Couple of days ago."

He's calculating.

"She still on the gear then?"

Sometimes she fucking hates Trevor. "Well?"

"No Trevor she's not on the gear."

The car slows to a stop, as he pulls off the road. She wonders if he is going to drag her out and give her a kicking. She knows she deserves it. She wouldn't fancy it much if she'd not had the last couple of days to cope with. She likes the idea even less now. She zips her jacket up, in preparation. Trevor turns to look at her.

"We're gonna have to buy this boy back from them Turks OK? You're paying, I'm talking. Who's his brother? Anton?"

"His cousin."

"What were you gonna do with him?"

They never take anyone on without having work for them to do.

"Dunno." Her eyes are downcast.

He looks at Sonny, incredulous. Dani takes a deep breath.

"Look. I get it. I fucked up."

He turns back to face the front.

"Maybe you've been *sharing* the fucking gear with her."

Sonny moves at the same time she does, throwing himself in front of her as she lunges forward, snarling.

"You fucking cunt! Don't fucking talk about her! What the fuck do you know?" She is spitting with rage. Sonny grabs her, climbing into the back almost on top of her. Trevor gets out of the truck.

"Let her go." He is perfectly calm as he walks around to her door. "Come on. Let her go."

"Get off me!"

She punches out at Sonny, dodging him in an effort to make eye contact with Trevor.

"Calm down." Sonny is hanging onto her arms desperately. He's no weakling, but her temper is wild as she kicks at the door. Trevor steps forward and opens it.

"I said, let her go."

Sonny has no choice, allowing Dani to struggle free and scramble out onto the street. Trevor waits until she straightens up, grabbing her by the throat and ramming her up against the side of the car. She lashes out, her fist hitting him on the side of the head. She may as well have slapped him with a wet tissue, for all the effect it has. He squeezes until he has her attention. She stops moving. She stares at him, refusing to blink. Refusing to show she is in pain.

Sonny has to look the other way.

"Now you fucking listen to me carefully." Trevor's voice is low, menacing.

"I don't give a fuck what this girl is doing to you. If me or Sonny or any of the boys have to go to war with the Turks because of you, I'm gonna send her myself. You understand? Now get in the fucking car!"

She gasps when he lets go. She refuses to let her hand go to her throat, climbing sullenly into the back.

They drive in silence to the yard to pick up one of the trucks and some overalls for the other two.

"We'll have to go by ourselves. Don't want the boys knowing you've lost your mind."

Trevor looks her directly in the eye when he says this, daring her to respond, but she picks her overalls off the seat and bites her tongue. She goes into the office, locks her phone and keys in her desk drawer and puts the overalls on. She takes her trainers off, replacing them with a pair of walking boots. They don't belong to anyone specific. She keeps the cash in her pocket.

She meets them by one of the trucks. They are similarly dressed. There is one phone between them that Sonny has recently borrowed from an aunt. Any problems, she can report it lost or stolen.

Sonny calls the Turks. He speaks to Ayrton's brother Hassan and he hangs up, turning towards Dani, who is staring across the yard.

"We might have to pay for what they lost as well."

"Fucking stronging it a bit ain't they?"

It's the first time she's spoken in almost an hour.

"Well they know we won't want this to get out, don't they?"

"Yeah I get it." Her throat still hurts.

"Look I'm with ya, OK? That's just how it is."

When did Sonny get so grown up and sensible? She turns to look at him and then at Trevor who is standing apart. They've all known each other a long time. Long enough for Dani to know Trevor is an inch away from giving her the kicking she knows she deserves.

She needs to get hold of herself and start thinking straight, right now, but all she can think about is the fact she's got Susanna back. Can it really be true? Trevor can kick her all the way around the North Circular if he wants to, but Dani is not giving up Susanna for anyone or anything. The fact is, she couldn't if she wanted to – and she doesn't want to.

In Dani's flat, Susanna is still waiting. She's called work and taken the day as holiday but had to speak to her manager Beverley in person, to reassure her it wasn't owing to a relapse. She's asked Sophie to take time off as well and she's on the way over to Dani's. Half an hour has passed and unused to being there alone, she wanders around, trying to stop herself prying. She cleans up the broken glass, shaking her head as she thinks about their tangled lives.

She has never seen Marie, although she's been told she looks like a model. Bitch. She chalks it up as a point in her favour when she sees there are no pictures of the famous Marie in the flat.

In the living room there's a picture of Joshua, the first long-term girlfriend's son. Susanna knows there is no threat here. She knows Dani has a good relationship with Sarah, now strictly platonic. Their relationship was neutralised long ago when Susanna met Dani by chance, out shopping. Sarah had been Dani's rebound relationship after their split.

She smiles at the memory of Dani as a teenager. Head bowed, hands always shoved deep in her jeans pockets. She always had half a cigarette tucked behind her ear and gold rings on most of her fingers. She remembers the look on Dani's face as she walked towards her on the high street that day.

She was so cocky even then, taking her time, looking at Susanna's body long and hard before making eye contact. She was never subtle,

"Can we go to your house?"

She'd said this with a big smile on her face as if she'd already got the answer she wanted. In response, Susanna had adopted the tone a schoolteacher would use with an unruly pupil.

"Hello, Dani. How are you?" she'd said coolly, trying to emphasise Dani's lack of sophistication. She wonders now if Dani picked up on that. If she had, she didn't care and answered, "Horny. Let's go to your place."

"No."

"Come on. I want to talk to you."

"You just said you were horny."

"Yeah." She'd laughed, silently. "I still want to talk to you."

Susanna had smiled.

"What about?"

"About how you look in that dress."

She couldn't help but flirt right back. She knew Dani had a new girlfriend and was pleased it wasn't serious. She'd not wanted to leave Dani in the first place.

They went to Susanna's. She recalls she'd started crying and how Dani held her and stroked her until she calmed down. She'd stayed and cooked chicken and rice for her, leaving the cooking only to sit and hold her. Dani hadn't known of her growing addiction to cocaine at that time – the first time they'd admitted they were in love. Susanna knew then it was only a matter of time before the end of Dani's relationship with Sarah.

She stops abruptly, getting quickly to her feet. Above the stereo is a picture of Dani holding a little girl. Her stomach twists in knots at the proud look on Dani's face. The little girl is slim, so slim and very cute, she has to admit it. It's not just the look on Dani's face that bothers her, but the way the child has her arms wrapped so tightly around Dani's neck. It makes her want to empty the dustpan full of broken glass into her mouth and chew it up until she can feel no more.

Susanna's nagging feeling of wanting a child has gradually become an incessant ache. She can barely think of anything else. She'd given more than a passing thought to the idea of having a baby with Carly. She would never tell Dani that of course. It's just that she'd come to the point of feeling she had to accept she was never really going to get Dani – not the way she wanted anyway. And somehow the idea of relapsing while in a relationship with Carly hadn't felt so petrifying.

Last night's events are still a little blurred in her mind. She feels like a teenager now, waiting for the phone call after that first time, hoping it is not just a one-night stand. She tries to imagine what the baby she'd have with Dani would look like. Who would the donor be?

She goes out on the landing to throw the glass down the chute. Then she goes back inside, walking to the bedroom. She bends to sneak a look in the drawer by the bed. She has no idea what she expects to find. She opens the drawer slowly, gingerly until she sees her own handwriting. It's a letter she'd sent when she was in rehab. It was the first day she had been allowed to communicate with the outside world. Dani was the only person she contacted.

As she sank down on the bed with the contents of the drawer, she saw the cinema tickets, chopsticks from their favourite restaurant, the cards, everything. It was all there. She herself had saved nothing, her once chaotic lifestyle erasing much of their early time together. But Dani had saved it all. The drawer was full.

She read the letter. In it she'd explained the reasons they needed to stay apart. She saw the stock recovery phrases: "need to take responsibility … need to do it for myself … need to avoid high risk situations" She smiled, shaking her head fondly. Dani. Her very own personal high-risk situation.

There was a photograph of Susanna that Dani had taken when they were in the park together. Cross-legged on the bed, holding it with both hands, she studied the picture. Her hair had been long and permed then. It looked awful. She saw herself smiling at the camera, winking cheekily. They hadn't yet slept together.

Dani had been relentless in her pursuit but it took months before Susanna gave in. She remembered the picture was taken on the day she'd decided she was going to have sex with her …

It had been a dull, grey, Thursday afternoon. Dani was eighteen, Susanna twenty-two. Susanna was teaching art and design at the college one day each week, whilst completing her PhD. Dani was failing at her sports course. Susanna taught once during the day and again the same evening so had the whole afternoon free until the second lecture. As she'd planned to take pictures of the lake that afternoon, she'd agreed to meet Dani at the park. She carried a camera with her often then. She'd forgotten that.

The photo of Susanna was the only one taken that day, as the light was so bad. And the picture was taken from the side because they'd been sitting at an outdoor table. It was the type with benches attached either side. Dani, she remembered, didn't sit opposite her, straddling the same side as Susanna instead, facing her profile. She'd picked up Susanna's camera. She smiles, remembering the way she'd tried to avoid Dani's gaze. Eventually though she'd looked at the camera to appease her and Dani clicked the shutter.

"Why are you so beautiful, Susanna?" So direct it was disarming.

"You smoke too much." She'd tried to maintain some sort of dignity.

"You know I can't sleep cos of you."

Susanna had turned to face her again.

"Why don't you try going home instead of clubbing every night?"

"You think I'm out clubbing every night?"

"I know you are. I can see the dark circles round your eyes."

"I'm out every night trying to find where you live."

"What?"

She didn't care.

"Is your bedroom at the back?"

"No, but the police station's local."

Dani had laughed.

"You think I'm joking."

It turned out she wasn't.

"Is that how you behave?"

"I'm desperate."

"I don't sleep with women."

"I told you, I just want to kiss you."

"Why?"

"Because that's what happens in my dreams."

Susanna had looked skywards, blushing.

"It's not gonna happen Dani, so please give it up."

"Just one kiss?"

"Why can't we be friends?"

"OK, come clubbing with me tomorrow."

"A gay club?"

Dani spread her hands. Where else?

"As a friend?"

"Yeah."

"I'm bringing someone with me."

"Yeah, bring him. We'll leave him in the men's section."

"Ha ha. A woman."

"Fine."

"So you wouldn't mind if I brought a man?"

"It's whether he'd mind watching us kiss."

Susanna had rolled her eyes, trying not to smile. "I'm not kissing you."

"Have you never kissed a friend?"

"Not the way you want to kiss me."

Dani smiled at that. Susanna had looked away. Dani moved in closer, dropping her voice.

"What's so special about the way I wanna kiss you Suse?"

It was the first time she had ever called her that. Susanna found she couldn't look at Dani then. She was blushing again. No answer.

Dani was in full flow by now, the volume of her voice dropping even further as she moved ever closer.

"When I day-dream about you, it's slow and it's warm," she'd whispered. "You're stroking my neck."

Susanna recalled she'd looked down at the table.

"It's different in my real dreams though ..."

Dani wasn't smiling when Susanna finally turned to look at her and lifted one leg, then the other free of the bench. She'd stood up – and walked away.

Dani had waited for her after the evening class. Susanna expected another apology. Instead Dani handed her a flyer.

"I'll see you later."

She'd left her then, but Susanna glimpsed the smile was back on Dani's face.

Susanna lies back on Dani's bed, remembering how back at their flat, she'd told Sophie they were going clubbing on the gay scene. Sophie had given her a "who are you kidding?" look. Susanna had been telling her all along it was ridiculous to suggest she'd even consider spending time with the young, cocky Dani.

"Come on. It'll be fun,' Susanna had urged. "We can call the girls and make a night of it." Sophie agreed eventually, although Susanna knew her reckless side sometimes had Sophie worried.

Four of them had gone to the club. Her friends had worn jeans but Susanna had put on a short, velvet, clingy, black dress. She grinned at the memory of Sophie's raised eyebrows when she saw her come out of her room.

They'd been in the club for about half an hour, when Susanna felt a hand on her wrist. She had been walking past a darkened corner and was pulled gently into it. Her eyes took a while adjusting, but she knew it was her. Who else?

She walked blindly into Dani's arms and found herself in a slow dance. It was the first time she had seen Dani out of her customary jeans and suede jacket. That night she was wearing a black shirt with black trousers. She seemed to stand more erect. She looked taller. They said nothing as they danced, while poor Sophie looked around confused. Where could Susanna have gone? She'd been right behind her.

They danced through four songs because Dani wouldn't let her go. Susanna heard her breathing change as she began teasing her, pressing against her, allowing her arms to slip around her neck. Eventually Dani had raised her head from her shoulder and waited until Susannah did the same.

"Can we go now?" It was almost a whisper.

Susanna bit her lower lip.

Throughout the years, this would be the gesture that always sent Dani into orbit, she'd confessed. She'd also told Susanna how she'd fought to hold onto her patience, actually wanting to drag her out of the club. How she was tired of talking, persuading as she'd run her hand up Susanna's back, just making her pain worse.

"Let's go." Dani had said, but it came out more a plea than a command.

She took Susanna home in a car she'd apparently stolen specifically for that night. Susanna's hand shook as she unlocked her door. She'd looked back at Dani to see her staring again, the cocky bravado replaced by anticipation. She led Dani straight to her room, not wanting to be disturbed by Sophie when she returned.

"Do you want a drink?"

Dani was standing with her back against the wall.

"Come here."

"Just one kiss, remember?"

Dani had smiled slyly and Susanna recalled saying, "Why don't I trust you?"

"It's better if you come to me." She'd indicated the bed behind Susanna.

Susanna had bitten at her lip again. Immediately, Dani had moved toward her, pushing her down onto the bed.

Susannah remembers kissing her for the first time, how she stopped to look at Dani's face. She'd asked herself if she felt strange or that it was wrong. No. She'd wondered if she'd regret what she was about to do. Probably. But she'd allowed Dani to kiss her again and hadn't stopped her when she began touching her. She helped remove her dress. She giggled as Dani tried unsuccessfully to undo her bra …

For the second time that day she hears banging at the door. She jumps up smiling. Seeing the memorabilia of their relationship in the drawer has made her feel nostalgic. Sophie is the best person to talk to about Dani. She's seen it all.

She flings open the door in triumph, ready to announce she's finally got her girl. But it's not Sophie.

A tall, dark, beautiful woman stands in front of her, curling her lip. Susanna recognises the child with her from the photo in the living room.

11

Saddle Up

Dani has finally managed to get her breathing under control. She can still feel burning on the side of her throat where Trevor's gargantuan thumb is no doubt still imprinted.

She's slumped low in the back so he can't see her eyes in his rearview mirror. Strange as it seems she hasn't seen him angry that often. Oh, she's seen him scowl and bare his teeth, rear up making himself taller and wider in intimidation mode. But she knows him well enough to see through the performance. Trevor can select whichever character he chooses out of his toolbox and discard it without a moment's thought, once it ceases to have the desired effect. He'll just go through them until he gets what he wants.

She's staring out the window as they drive along. The silence has given her time to think. She is not the type to sulk, rather she'll try to step back from the situation and analyse it rationally. She's good at that, skilled. She could have such a different life if her emotions didn't come crashing in at the most crucial times and tip everything off balance. She sneaks a look at the back of Sonny's head. He too is staring out of the window. He's obviously disappointed in her but he's still loyal. Trevor's angry with her but again he's still here. He could have left her to it.

She'll tackle him first.

"Trevor."

"What?"

He answers mildly as if he hasn't just tried to squeeze the life out of her in the middle of the high street.

"I'm into her. You understand? Properly. I'm just telling you lot straight, now. No more fucking about."

They both glance back at her. Trevor pulls out of the traffic again. He brings the truck to a stop, kills the engine and turns his whole body in the seat to look at her.

Dani takes a deep breath. She hates this. She never talks to anyone about Susanna.

"I know all the crazy stuff I used to do over her. It's not gonna be like that, this time. No more madness." She shifts in the seat, avoiding both their eyes. "I want her back."

They both wait poker-faced, as she mutters, "I shouldn't have done that with Dennis. I'm sorry. But I really needed to find her, quick." Her voice fades away, embarrassed at the force with which she's spoken. She shrugs. "Otherwise I'd have lost her for good."

Trevor grimaces at the thought that they were that close to being rid of this girl. He'd tried to threaten her to stay away in the past but she'd been too off her head to see who or maybe what was standing in front of her at the time and laughed in his face. He seethes at the memory. Feeling the tension Dani adds quickly, "However Dennis got in the back of that van, it's on me. I owe him because he wouldn't be in

London if I never brought him down here. He's gonna be my pet project for three months. If it doesn't work out after that, then I'll put him on a train home myself."

Trevor's not convinced.

"If he's had a hand in that truck job, that's not on us, is it? Did you hear what I said? He was probably gonna come down anyway."

"Yeah but I gave him a reason to be here. It might have been the thing that persuaded him."

Trevor is shaking his head, but Dani is patient.

"Look, he's not a bad kid."

"What – like Marvin?"

"Yeah, just like him."

"Well he needs to choose his friends better."

Dani nods, thinking. "Colin." She's shaking her head now, "That's what he meant about me looking after my soldiers."

Trevor's tone is grim.

"Couple of years ago, we'd have be talking about sending him on a one-way trip for talking to you like that."

Sonny quickly interjects.

"Hold on! Lets leave that kinda talk for another day."

Trevor is giving Dani a meaningful look.

"No, that Colin ... I ain't arguing on that little shit's behalf. He's already taken the piss with us."

Sonny doesn't like the direction they're heading in.

"We're trying to put a full stop on this, not start a new war."

Trevor is still not happy.

"Who's gonna fight for that little shit? Geezer like that, his own mum will forget him by tomorrow."

Dani nods in agreement.

"Sonny's right, though. But Colin's only got one more life

left with me. And another thing, we ain't paying the Turks extra."

Sonny sighs. Fuck.

"Dani, I'm trying to get us all home tonight."

"I know." She raises her hands in surrender. "I shouldn't have got us into this, but trust me. I'll be careful." She talks over his objections. "I ain't completely lost my mind. I know what I see when I look at them Turks. If we just give them what they want they'll only keep pushing for more. We never fucking took their truck did we? They know that but they're just tryna take advantage cos they know we value our reputation."

Trevor snorts.

"Dani you're the only one that gives a fuck about all that reputation shit. They want their money."

"Yeah. And they'll get it, but not from us."

She's gaining confidence as her brain gradually finds its way out of the fog that is Susanna. "I don't think they really believe we're involved in stealing their truck. They know we wouldn't have known about it. Why d'you think they called us in the first place? It's cos we're known for being on the level. They're gonna try ain't they? If we were a bunch of mugs ..." She wags a finger, "or if we really did know about it, we'd pay wouldn't we?"

"I hope you're right."

"I am Trev."

He breathes in through his nostrils.

"We better get going."

Trevor's expression suggests he's winding himself up. Sonny, resigned to the fact that he'll be the only voice of reason tonight, turns back to face the front. A mile out, Trevor decides to change the route in.

"Instinct," he says in response to their quizzical looks. "We weren't a part of the problem before, but you could say we might end up that way depending how you look at it."

They nod. He's right.

"Give us that phone, Sonny," he says. Both look at him again. "They know we're coming alone don't they? That ain't a good feeling."

He calls Mikey as it begins to dawn on each of them just how much of a difficult position Dani may have got them in. When he hangs up he turns to her.

"You need to talk for as long as possible. It's gonna take the soldiers an hour to get there at least. We can't go in late cos it will look hot. Sonny, you text if we need to call them off, alright? Everyone knows you're always on the phone during a Meet."

His speech is increasing in tone and speed as he prepares for battle.

"You got anything on ya, Dani?"

"Nah."

"Here, have this."

He places a gun in her hand. Shit. That focuses her mind.

"You come to my house with that today?"

"Don't be silly."

She thinks about Susanna, the luxury of seeing her when she returns home.

"No. I don't want it."

"Dani we ain't neutral tonight."

"Yeah, I know. I don't need it. I can do this."

"Sonny?"

"No, me neither."

Trevor nods grimly. It's fine by him. He's the only one with that type of experience, anyway.

He pulls over and goes into a West Indian takeaway, returning with three Guinness punches and six patties. They eat and drink hungrily, smoking a spliff each. This had been a ritual in the old days. She smiles at each of them, feeling much better now.

"Do I need to say sorry again?"

She's looking at Sonny in particular. He's been mostly quiet. He looks sideways at her, squinting through the smoke.

"This is the one then?"

"The one what?"

"The girl," he says, waving his spliff at her.

"Oh, yeah." She's past feeling embarrassed. She smiles. "It's like Sweets says, I wasn't doing nothing crazy over anyone else, cos they didn't really matter."

Trevor talks with his mouth full.

"Fuckin 'ell. She must be good for you to let Marie go!"

"You're thinking with your dick, Trev."

"Yeah, cos I can. What you thinking with?"

"It ain't like that. She looks good but she doesn't ... she doesn't make me wanna ... I dunno. My Suse, when I look at her, Marie and everyone else just fades out. It's always been like that with her."

Sonny speaks.

"She ain't that bad looking though."

"My Suse?" Dani sighs. "I don't know what everyone else sees, but I just can't leave her alone."

"Not like that wossername on the telly eh?"

They all have a sharp intake of breath and laugh.

"I'd do her."

"I'd go second."

"Sonny!"
They're laughing out loud.
"Would you go after me, Dani?"
"I'd go after the fucking soldiers!"
They are cracking up, elbowing each other. They're ready now. *Saddle up.*

12

My Suse

Susanna stands in the doorway looking at the impeccably dressed Marie. In contrast, she's wearing yesterday's crumpled dress, one of Dani's sweat tops and a pair of slippers. Added to that, the colour has drained from her face. Little Jessica runs straight past her, down the hallway and disappears into the bedroom.

"Dani?"

The two women stare at each other. Marie is confused. She's come here to have an argument today and perhaps threaten to end the relationship. Dani's sudden absence from her life has come as a shock, and Marie cannot – will not – accept it. Dani has always been reliable in her own way, and it has angered Marie that she could abandon Jessica in the way she has. Marie has always had a sneaking suspicion Dani's feelings for Jessica were stronger than those for her. Her treatment of Jessica, who adores her, is not going to be easily forgiven.

She wonders if the girl standing in front of her is a friend's girlfriend or relative. Dani is always helping some waif or stray but Marie would have appreciated being told a woman was staying in her flat. Perhaps that's what Dani wanted to speak to her about. She knows Dani's no cheat, but still she's tired of her crap. She's also annoyed at Dani's inability to include her in her life. Marie almost never comes here, but Dani keeps a spare key at her house, which she's brought with her today. It would've served this girl right if she'd walked straight in.

She's not confident enough of her sexuality to declare herself as Dani's girlfriend, so she introduces herself simply.

"I'm Marie."

She's hoping Dani has bothered to mention her, but it is the girl's reaction that sounds an alarm. She avoids Marie's eyes.

"She – she's not here."

Marie's eyes narrow.

"Where is she?"

"Um." Susanna has pulled the track top across her chest. "She had to go somewhere with Sonny and Trevor."

Well, she knows the cronies then, thinks Marie, looking at Dani's sweat top the girl is wearing.

"Where?"

Susanna shrugs.

"She wouldn't tell me." The second she says it Susanna realises she's told Marie all she needs to know.

Marie holds her temper. Instead, she says coldly,

"Get used to it." And then, "Excuse me."

She steps past Susanna who is now holding her head.

"Shit! Shit!" She claps her hand to her forehead as Marie walks down the hallway,

"Jessica, come. We're going."

"Mummy, I want Dani."

She follows the sound of her daughter's voice into the bedroom. Susanna waits in the hallway, praying silently for

Sophie to arrive. Why does being in Dani's life always carry the side effect of feeling like a whore? There is silence from the bedroom that seems to last too long.

"Oh shit!" Susanna moans with the realisation of the reason for this.

She edges tentatively to the open bedroom door, to see Marie looking down at the mementoes she's left strewn across the bed. Marie is holding a picture face down in her hand. The date is on the back.

Susanna steps slowly backwards. If she hasn't seen me, I can just …

"Who are you?" snaps Marie.

Susanna freezes, neither in nor out of the bedroom. She wants to say, "I'm the reason Dani will never love you. Dani can't love you because of me." She wants to say "I've waited for years for her, so you and your pretty little daughter may as well leave now, because I'm not going anywhere."

"I'm Susanna," she says, stepping fully into the room.

This means nothing to Marie. She can see that. Marie looks around the room, suddenly embarrassed there is nothing she can pick up and storm out with. Only Jessica. A wave of pain and humiliation hits her. Her head feels light. Still sitting on the bed, she looks up at Susanna.

"How long have you been here?"

Susanna has no intention of answering her. She looks towards the door, unsure if she wants Sophie to witness this. Jessica is now by her mother, holding her hand.

"Where Dani?"

Marie stands, letting the photo drop onto the bed.

"Tell her I'll leave her things out by the bins. She can collect them if she wants."

She stalks out past Susanna, taking care not to brush

– 163 –

against her.

Exhaling loudly as the front door slams, Susanna sinks down once more onto the bed and reaches for the photograph Marie had been holding. She sees an image of herself in Dani's hallway, wearing nothing but Dani's favourite shirt. She's standing, rubbing the sleep out of her eyes with a shy smile. On the back is the date, summer last year. Underneath the date, Dani has written "My Suse".

Again, there's knocking at the front door, but this time she uses the spy-hole before opening it. Sophie has a huge grin on her face and coffee and croissants in her hands.

"I know how hungry you get after sex!"

Susanna smiles tentatively.

"I think I might have just got rid of the competition as well."

"What have you done?"

"Quick, come in before she comes back."

Susanna shuts the door. Sophie's eyes are wide.

"She was here?"

"Don't! I thought she was gonna beat the crap out of me."

"What did you say to her?"

"I swear I didn't mean to."

"Yeah, like at the pool club that time."

Sophie follows her into the flat.

"No, honestly. She's one scary lady."

"Susanna! You two have to sort this out. Carly went mental the other night."

"I think we have … No properly, this time," she says, looking back at Sophie's cynical expression. "No more crazy stuff. And I'll speak to Carly."

"Hmmm. I'll believe that when I see it."

Susanna is smiling now. "Don't tell Dani I showed you this."

She walks to the bedroom and points to the bed.

"Wow!" Sophie drops the croissants on the bed, handing the coffees to Susanna. "How old is this picture?"

"Look on the back. And look at this."

"OK, you officially have your stalker back."

"Shut up, Sophie! And don't get your crumbs all over it."

There's another photograph of the two of them together, which Sophie hands to Susanna. She laughs.

"Hey, I think I took this one ..."

13

Five, six, seven, eight …

They drive through a stone arch and park in the courtyard. The Meet is inside a cardboard factory in Highgate. There are no suits today, instead they're bulked up with clothes under the overalls.

Paul greets them, shaking their hands. He raises an eyebrow at their dress but none of them offers an explanation as they're led inside to tables set up at the far end of the floor. Dani can see no other exits.

Ayrton's already seated. He shakes their hands, rising just enough to reach each of them. Paul sits next to him, so they take their own seats. Sonny was about to take one of the seats at the head of the table as they always do, but Dani has sat down opposite Paul. Sonny and Trevor exchange glances but sit either side of her anyway. Maybe she has a reason for doing that. Maybe she wants Colin in the middle of the two camps in order to intimidate him. The reality is that Dani's head is not quite here yet. She's thinking about Susanna's fingers tangled in her hair, her nails running down Dani's back. She blinks, trying her best to focus on the task at hand.

"Who we waiting on?"

Trevor indicates plenty of empty seats around the table. "Your lot."

"It's just us," says Dani.

"Your boy John's just called to say he's on his way."

Trevor clenches his jaw.

"We never called him," says Sonny.

"You having communication problems Dani?"

Paul peers at her over the bottle of water he is draining. She acts unconcerned.

"It's just a loyalty thing, no big deal."

"If you say so."

Trevor, Sonny and Dani resist the urge to make eye contact with each other. Something's not right here. What's John playing at?

Paul's phone rings and he goes to the door, letting in John, Whisky, Simon, Abdi … Dani's wondering how John got Paul's number when the final member of the group enters. Carly – wearing a suit …

Dani's teeth clamp down in her mouth, her temples pulsing. What the fuck is she doing here!

She once had to attend an anger management course. It was the alternative to a short prison sentence for assaulting a police officer who'd tried to search Susanna. Apparently you have to focus on the problem rather than the person, then count yourself up from anger to composure. But what if the person *is* the fucking problem?

Immediately, Dani starts counting in her head. One, two, three four, five, six, seven eight, nine, ten, breathe. She uses the time it takes the newcomers to cross the room, to adjust her expression. She looks neither left nor right. Just straight at Carly.

Sonny's brow knits in confusion while Trevor looks skyward. He should have said something to Johnny the first time he brought his sister along. He knew something wasn't right about it. Now he realises this girl has it in for Dani. She's gonna do something in retaliation for that fucking Susanna.

Dani slows her breathing. She can't let her dispute with Carly distract her. Besides, Susanna is hers. She always has been.

Eleven twelve, thirteen … She holds out her hand.

"How's it going?"

Carly looks her straight in the eye, very calm.

"I'm not shaking your hand."

"Why not?" Dani asks innocently. "You know where it's been."

"Fuck off!"

Dani sneers. Not so calm now, are we? She takes a quick look at Paul and Ayrton. Their blank expressions suggest they are unaware of the dispute between Carly and herself.

Dani turns to the others, ignoring the murderous looks from Carly.

"Where's these boys then?"

John sits and the others, including Carly, follow. There's silence as Paul hands plastic bottles of water around, while everyone eyes each other suspiciously.

Then there's a sudden banging at the metal shutter and Paul gets up to see who it is. Dani notes both Trevor and Ayrton have the same reaction to the noise, their hands moving immediately to their breast pockets. Trevor was right.

Colin walks – no, swaggers in – alone. Dani can see the

we'll empty clips in you first before we decide who's next."

Trevor closes his eyes. Now that her temper is running the show, there's no telling what she'll say next. It's bad enough that she's turned what was supposed to be a negotiation into a personal sparring match, but on top of that, she's now told the Turks that Trevor is armed.

But Dani is oblivious. She glares again over at Carly.

"It'll be Colin first then whoever I don't fucking like."

Again she rounds on Colin.

"If you wanna run soldiers, you're gonna get this boy back, cos if you don't everyone will know you left him high and dry and you'll have problems getting anyone to do anything for ya."

Colin's eyes flicker to John. She can see he's irritated with himself for allowing her to see that.

"What? You think these guys are gonna sell me out over a girl?"

She's guessed correctly that Carly and John have made it clear Dani is not in their good books at the moment. She adds bad-mouthing her around to her mental list of wrongs done by Carly and John. She snarls at Carly.

"I know John never came here to talk about my sex life."

She can't resist baiting Carly. She has completely lost control of herself. She turns to Ayrton, and says by way of explanation, "She's crying cos she found out I'm doing her girl."

Carly stands up suddenly, fuming. Dani glares up at her, unconcerned at any physical threat she may be considering.

"Sit down, we're working here."

She dismisses her with a flick of her hand and turns away but Carly remains standing, disgusted that Dani would speak about Susanna in that way. Dani turns back to her, smiling nastily as she prepares to destroy her with her next remark.

But Carly is ready for her,

"I'm not staying in the same room as her. Anyway, there's someone I need to speak to." She looks meaningfully at Dani. "What's the quickest way to Hornsey?"

Dani feels the room sway as beads of sweat appear suddenly on her forehead. She knows where I live! One, two, three, Fuck! Fuck! Four, five, breathe … Her dominance collapses. She turns to Sonny, her jaw clenched, nostrils flaring.

He knows she wants to get up and tie Carly to a chair, smash her hands, break her legs, anything to keep her away from Susanna. Dani visualises jumping up and grabbing Carly by the throat. She should have taken that gun. She'd be pushing it in her fucking mouth now. At the same time Trevor is thanking God she refused it. He knows she would have used it. He holds his breath.

Dani can hear Susanna telling her she what? She cares for her? She can't help thinking of Susanna's hands on Carly's back. Six, seven, eight, nine, ten, breathe. The anger has become a physical pain in her chest. She looks at Carly, smiling down at her and they both know Carly has her just where she wants her. Dani fights to bring herself under control. The last thing she needs is the Turks getting all inquisitive about where she lives.

Carly exhales contentedly.

When they initially met, Susanna had made it clear to Carly she had no plans to start a relationship and tried her best to explain the situation with Dani. But Carly had fallen for Susanna almost immediately, the vulnerability irresistible to her.

She'd tried to be patient, believing that in time Susanna would get over her ex girlfriend. She was willing to listen when

Susanna talked about Dani until she began to realise that was *all* she talked about. She heard about things Dani had done in the past and it rankled that Susanna always found ways to excuse her behaviour. She couldn't understand why the thing between them just wouldn't die. But what she did know was that jealousy played a huge part in Dani's relationship with Susanna. Carly wasn't sure if she was ready to have children in her life, but she was willing to bet that it was the one thing that would break Dani and Susanna apart forever.

Susanna had described Dani as being head over heels in love with her, passionate and jealous. Carly saw instead an arrogant, unbalanced bully. She saw no evidence of Dani having any love for Susanna. To Carly it seemed as though Dani liked to show others she could force Susanna into submission whenever she chose.

Carly had turned up at the previous Meet to get an idea of what she was up against. She didn't think Dani was all that special. Not like everyone was saying. Anyone could do that with all those guys behind her. She'd encouraged her twin brother to attend this Meet, knowing Dani would have no choice but to stay. That way she could be free to go and try to talk some sense into Susanna. She'd promised John she wouldn't cause any trouble, and now he was firing warning looks at her. Well, he can't leave either. She feels bad for tricking him like that but she just couldn't stand by and let Dani get away with it. She knows he'll be really pissed off when he finds out she went behind his back and contacted Colin. She actually thinks Colin is a horrible little geezer, but they have a hatred of Dani in common. Listening to him today it seems Colin hates everyone but right now he's an ally.

She would never forget the way Susanna had left the club with Dani. John had them followed. She was so distraught that night he would have done anything for her.

Worse still, Susanna didn't answer her calls until the next night and when they met up she said she'd spent the night with Dani. She didn't even lie about it! She was crying, talking about how she was sorry and really didn't want to go back but she had to. It made no sense! She swore Dani hadn't threatened her or harmed her in any way, yet she kept saying she didn't want to go back, but she would.

Not if Carly could help it.

"I'll tell her you said 'Hi', shall I?"

Carly turns and walks slowly to the exit. She can feel Dani's eyes burning into her shoulder blades as she deliberately takes her time, stringing out the agony. She knows the Turks are not going to let Dani just walk out of their Meet over some girl drama. They want their money and by the looks on their faces they're gonna start kicking off soon if someone doesn't start talking numbers to them.

Trevor and Sonny hold their breath. Dani is gripping the chair handles, squirming inside, unable to count any further. She can feel their anxiety. That has never happened before. In the last few weeks, it seems she's managed to destroy all the trust she's spent years building with them. Paul and Ayrton are both staring at her. It's clear no one else is going anywhere. She has no choice but to stay. If she tries to leave, all hell will break loose.

She sucks in air, clamping her mouth shut, as the door opens.

Colin's eyes are gleaming maliciously.

"Hold on a minute Carly." He smiles an evil smile at her. "Just answer one question and you can go."

Carly frowns, not sure where he's going with this. Trevor glowers. This is all getting out of hand. He doesn't want to hear even one more word out of Dani. He'll take care of this. He turns to Colin.

"You paying these geezers or what?"

Paul's patience has run out.

"Look, if no one claims this boy he's gonna fucking disappear."

Dani's focus snaps back into the room. She is not sure if he's bluffing. Hard to tell with him. She sits back and raises her hands. "He ain't ours."

Whisky frowns.

"Fucking hell Dani!"

Her brain is slowly clicking back into gear. Admitting Dennis is hers is the same as accepting responsibility for the truck job. She repeats,

"He ain't ours."

Paul is beginning to turn a funny colour.

"He's yours or his."

He points at Colin. But Dani is adamant.

"My boys don't go around jacking trucks."

She looks back at Colin.

"Today's the day you're gonna learn something about yourself. If you can't take control of your greed, you're gonna walk out of here with your throat exposed. Now you'll pay and you'll fucking get that boy back cos I've got other shit to deal with tonight."

She throws a look of pure hatred over at Carly, who is standing hesitantly at the door. She just wants to get out of here.

Colin ignores Dani, instead looking directly at Paul. His tone changes for the first time. He smiles wide.

"You can have him. Put him to work. That'll be payment for the truck."

Dani, Trevor and Sonny exchange worried, confused glances.

Ayrton raises an eyebrow.

"So it was you that took my truck?'

Colin nods.

"I ain't giving you no money though. I only did it cos Dennis asked me to help him. It was his job. He's her soldier." He inclines his head towards a startled Dani. "She's the one that owes you."

Ayrton nods darkly.

"Is that right?'

Dani's eyes are wide.

"Wait a sec …"

But Colin's deadpan tone returns as he raises a hand in her direction.

"I ain't talking to you."

Trevor snarls.

"So you'd do a job with Dennis one day and then sell him down the swanny the next?"

Colin replies, unconcerned. "Didn't you hear me just say he belongs to the Turks now?"

Paul and Ayrton exchange looks while Dani stands outraged.

"You ain't fucking selling him to no one!"

Colin is smiling triumphantly when he turns to face her.

"What do you care? I thought you said he weren't yours?"

Dani finds herself stammering.

"He – he's not mine, but you can't just …"

Colin sits up high in his chair. He's enjoying himself.

"I can prove he's yours."

Trevor is shaking his head. Sonny gets a text saying the soldiers are nearby, but he tells them to stay put. Things have taken an odd turn and he doesn't want to add any more fuel to the fire.

Dani glares, unsure of the correct response.

Colin turns to Paul.

"Now you know you can trust me." He indicates Dani. "She'll just look you in the eye and lie." Colin smiles cheekily. "You can put Dennis to work, but I'll work *with* ya."

Dani looks from Ayrton to Colin incredulously.

"You're not serious!"

Paul says it mildly.

"You be quiet, Dani."

Colin juts his chin out confidently.

"You won't be disappointed."

Again Ayrton and Paul exchange looks. Ayrton is confused.

"And exactly how is it we know we can trust you and not Dani?"

Colin looks as if he's won the lottery. He pushes his hand slowly down into his jeans pocket. Both Ayrton and Trevor have their guns out and pointed at him in an instant.

"Alright, alright." He's giggling like a child. "Let's not get silly."

Carly is edging slowly out of the door.

"Stay where you are!" Colin commands, the stupid smile gone from his face. "I just need you to tell them one thing then you can go."

Dani still cannot work out what is happening. Her brain is whirring with too much disconnected information. But then it all suddenly becomes clear when Colin shows his hand. He holds up a picture of Susanna.

Colin's eyes flash triumphantly.

"Just tell everyone who the girl in this picture is."

Dani feels a sickening jolt go through her body as Paul and Ayrton look from Carly to Colin quizzically.

Sonny looks to Trevor, bewildered. How are they gonna get out of this?

Colin couldn't be happier.

"See, I got this picture from Dennis. That's what he was working on, why he was in London. He was looking for this girl for Dani."

Now everyone is looking at Carly, Colin deals the final hammer blow.

"That's who you and Dani are fighting over ain't it?"

Susanna is lounging on the bed while Sophie makes phone calls. There is someone at the door – again. This time Susanna tiptoes to the spy-hole. The woman is vaguely familiar. She has shoulder length curly brown hair and large brown eyes. Susanna frowns, opening the door. The woman grins.

"Thought so."

Susanna raises an enquiring eyebrow at the woman's mischievous smile.

"You're Susanna aren't you?"

"Yes."

Sophie is standing behind her as the woman says, "Can I come in?"

Susanna puts her hands on her hips, jealousy jumping up in her eyes.

"Why don't you tell me who you are and we can go from there?"

The woman grins again, "You're just as bad as Dani. I'm Paula."

Susanna still refuses to step back.

"Trevor's wife."

"Oh!" Susanna is immediately ashamed. "I'm so sorry. Come in. I'm sorry. I didn't recognise you."

Paula walks to the living room, still grinning.

"Trevor told me to meet him here. He said I should check before letting myself in. They shouldn't be too much longer."

"Oh. Good."

The door knocks again just as she sits nervously opposite Paula. Susanna jumps to answer but Paula holds up a hand.

"How about I do it? Then you won't scare the right people off and let the wrong ones in."

She leaves the room before Susanna has a chance to respond. It's Sweets.

"Mikey's just parking. You might as well leave it open."

Paula grabs her arm, whispering conspiratorially.

"Guess who's here."

"Who?"

Susanna can hear them from inside the living room. She and Sophie exchange looks. Sweets comes into the room, looking her up and down.

"Susanna. How are you?"

There are more voices in the hallway. The flat is filling up faster than Susanna can remember all the names of those introduced to her. She looks over at Sophie, bewildered. She offers to get drinks but they're all helping themselves already.

Sweets leans over.

"I've just got a text from Sonny. It's gonna be a bit longer than they thought. He says we should just stay here."

Susanna nods. She's about to ask if everything is OK, but

Mikey walks in looking directly at her.
"There's someone at the door for ya."

Back in the workshop, Dani is deep in thought. She couldn't get her brain to work when Carly was first allowed to leave but seeing so many of the Turks' men entering the room is just what she needed to concentrate her mind. They're all trapped. She, Sonny, Trevor, Colin, Abdi, Simon, Whisky and Johnny. It's Johnny she's watching now. Carly may have found Dani's weak spot, but the way Dani sees it, so long as Johnny is here, Carly's position cannot be secure. But then, Dani thinks, it's unsettling that Carly wants Susanna so much that she would leave her brother here in this situation.

She understands now how Trevor and Sonny must feel, finding themselves in this position because of what Dani must have. But that's the truth isn't it? You can bend anyone into any shape you want if you know what they must have, can't you?

Now she switches her mind to Colin. So far, he's been clever, outsmarting everyone with his cunning plan. But he still has his weaknesses. Dani grimaces. Some people are the most vulnerable when they are winning. They're so happy the plan's actually coming together that they start congratulating themselves before they've collected the prize. People who are confident expose much more than those who are unsure.

And he's exposed his desire. Dani knows what he must have. He wants to step up to the big leagues. He wants it so desperately he's prepared to take huge risks to get there. He came alone, he admitted stealing from them. He's like a man with little to lose, believing that showing the Turks just how brave and ruthless he can be will impress them into taking him on. He's gone for it today. If he loses, he'll be nothing. He'll do anything for them. He'll sell his friends, his enemies, people like Whisky who he doesn't even know. He'll sell them all to get where he needs to go.

Dani nods. Now she knows how to break him.

There is no one neutral here. Everyone now has his own agenda. The Turks want their money and if they have to hurt everyone in here, they're gonna get it.

Dani, Sonny and Trevor need to preserve their, reputations, their money, maybe even their skin, but what about Whisky's boys? What are they even doing here?

If she could only suss that out she'd know how to approach them.

"So you're back?"

Sweets is appraising Susanna, who has just sat back down with a heavy sigh. Susanna nods slowly.

"That's the idea."

"Are you planning on sticking around this time?"

Sita says the last two words pointedly. Again Susanna nods.

"That's the plan."

Sweets ignores Paula who is nudging her to shut up.

"What's so different this time?"

Susanna looks her in the eye.

"I am." She looks up at the picture of Dani with Jessica. "Hopefully Dani is too."

Trevor is angry. He's so angry he could wring Dani's neck. Of course he'll take it out on Colin, but the mess Dani has got them in … He shakes his head, placing his gun on the table in front of him.

"Look." He addresses Ayrton. "I'll get your fucking money back. Just give me him for a couple of hours." Trevor reaches for Colin, who ducks away from his grasp.

"I told ya. It's not me that owes the money."

Ayrton shakes his head.

"I ain't gonna sit here watching everyone telling tales on everyone else …"

"But you need to," interjects Dani.

Paul moves around to where she is now standing. He pushes his face close up to hers.

"We don't give a fuck …"

"But you should." She interrupts again. "You know why?" She doesn't give him a chance to answer. "Cos if you take his word for it, you'll have someone on your crew that you don't know fuck all about."

Colin narrows his eyes. He doesn't want her to start putting doubts in their minds.

"It weren't me that lied to you lot about Dennis was it? Bring him in here he'll tell ya. Then she'll have to shut her mouth and go and get your money."

"Yeah bring him." She fires back. "You know what he'll tell ya? He'll tell ya he's met me once. He'll tell you he don't even know who these two are …" she indicates Sonny and Trevor on either side of her, "… and he'll tell you that this geezer …" she points at Colin, "… pulled him into a job then fucked him over so he could move up. He's already told you he don't give a fuck about no one. Why's he gonna suddenly start being loyal to you? When the law starts fucking putting it on him how long's it gonna take before he says one of your names?"

"I aint no fucking grass!"

"No? You grassed up Dennis to them didn't ya? Whether he's mine or yours that's what you did. Why you gonna be different with these guys? They're family, two families that made one, and now you think you're gonna walk in cos your willing to give people up?"

"I wouldn't …"

"No? Why not? You built your whole day on giving them Dennis. How do they know they ain't just another step for you?"

Back and forward they go until finally Colin shouts:

"Bring Dennis in here! Then you'll have to stop running your mouth."

"Yeah bring him!" Dani retorts.

Sonny's eyebrows hike but Dani knows she has no choice but to brazen it out.

Ayrton nods. Dani glares around the room as Hassan shouts out into the courtyard.

The boy that is eventually brought, almost carried in, is so battered and bruised Dani can barely tell if it's him. He is squinting painfully through swollen blacked eyes. He holds his broken wrist tightly against his chest. The pain is sapping his energy, giving him a greyish hue.

Paul laughs nastily.

"Come on in soldier boy."

A dishevelled mass of torn and bloody clothes, he moans, painfully shuffling further into the room. Dani shakes her head. Look at the state of him!

Paul is apparently oblivious to the horrified looks he's getting from around the room. He's only a kid for fucksakes.

"Coupla questions for ya then you can go alright?"

Dennis looks up mistrustfully into Paul's eyes.

"Who is this?" Paul points to Sonny.

Dennis' shoulders struggle with the effort of shrugging in reply.

"You don't know who this is?"

Dennis shakes his head, his eyes remaining downcast.

"So you're a soldier are ya?"

Dennis lowers his head even further.

"You're one of Dani's boys aren't ya?" Ayrton asks as if he's arranging a lunch date.

Dennis looks up then over at Dani. He swallows, dragging his dry tongue across chapped lips.

"A simple yes or no will do it," urges Paul. Fucking 'ell, he's just about had it with this lot today.

Dennis lowers his eyes again when he meets Trevor's blank gaze. Dani doesn't know they've met before.

Dennis shakes his head.

Dani holds herself taut.

"You don't know her?"

Again he shakes his head.

"Fucking liar!" Colin is about to get to his feet, but Sonny jumps up and steps in front, shielding Dennis. Paul frowns.

"I'm gonna give you one more chance. Now do you know her or not?"

Dennis looks up into Sonny's eyes before looking straight at Paul.

"I know who she is."

You could hear a pin drop. Paul breathes in through his nostrils.

"Oh yeah? Who is she?"

Dennis looks into Dani's eyes.

"She runs the soldiers. Looks after them."

"Do you work for her?"

He shakes his head.

"Why did you say you was a soldier?"

Dennis' lip quivers.

"To make you stop."

Dani swallows. It's sickening to watch.

Now Dennis' eyes harden as he makes eye contact with Colin.

"If I was working for her I wouldn't be here. I'm only here cos he set me up."

He points at Colin.

"He asked me to help him. He kept the money. I didn't get shit." He looks down at himself miserably.

Dani can take no more of this.

"Look. He's told you what you wanna know, now let him go." She shakes her head in disgust. "Look at the fucking state of him."

"Hold on," Ayrton barks. "I ain't done with him yet." He grabs Susanna's photograph from the table. Dennis flinches as Ayrton approaches him.

"I ain't gonna hurt ya."

Dennis is breathing heavily. It's as if one more blow is all it will take to break him permanently. Ayrton holds the picture close to Dennis' face. "You tell me who this is and you can walk out that door right now."

Paul chuckles to himself.

"I'm not sure he can mate."

"Shut up!"

It doesn't seem to Dani that there are many people that

can speak to Paul like that.

Whisky, John, Abdi and Simon have spent the whole time shrinking into their chairs, trying to be forgotten. Now they are staring at Dennis like everyone else in the room.

Dennis looks at the photo and then into Ayrton's eyes.

"And you'll let me go?"

Ayrton nods.

Dennis raises his chin ever so slightly despite the fact he's trembling.

"I wanna go, but I don't know her." Dani's jaw remains clenched as someone exhales audibly. Ayrton has suddenly come over all agreeable. He nods in Trevor's direction.

"You can all go now." He indicates Dennis. "Take him with you."

Dani knows this is not a good sign.

"Yeah." Paul chimes in. "No need to stick around. We'll take it from here."

His mild tone is not lost on them.

"Wait. Wait."

Dani's hands go to Trevor and Sonny's arms on either side, holding them in place. They can't just leave Colin there. She turns back to Ayrton. He seems less angry than Paul, though just as determined.

"You don't want me to get your money?"

Trevor gives her a look.

"Wait outside Dani."

She ignores him.

"Hang on. How much we talking?"

Ayrton takes his gun out and stands, walking around the table.

"Twenty? Twenty-five? Thirty? It don't matter now does it? He ain't paying it back. That's what you said isn't it?"

At last Colin starts to look nervous as Ayrton comes to stand behind him. He talks fast.

"I'll make you more than that. You'll see. I'm heartless! I can make nuff with you guys behind me."

Dani winces.

"Shut up Colin!"

But Paul drowns her out with unpleasant laughter.

"Oh." Paul's tone is mocking. "So all this is really just an audition?"

Trevor gets to his feet, gently moving Dani's hand from his shoulder.

"Dani, we're going."

Colin suddenly bolts from the chair, narrowly evading Ayrton's grasp. He yanks the door open, running out into the court-yard. Paul and Ayrton are laughing.

Dani's heart sinks. She knows he won't get far. She watches as Ayrton lets the picture of Susanna drop onto the table. Now he rubs his hands together in anticipation.

She hates losing, but more than that, she hates being made to watch the consequences of her failure. The Turks will make them all watch so that others are in no doubt as to what will happen to people who take the piss.

It's not long before they hear cries of pain. He's not holding back either. Colin is like those bad tempered wilful children who cry and scream the loudest, bang the hardest, all the while still refusing to back down. Dani clenches her jaw. She hates seeing violence. Whenever she metes it out herself, she lacks the presence of mind to fully take it in. Watching other people do it is just as distressing for her as for any helpless onlooker.

Colin is dragged in by his ankles, his head banging on the ground as he struggles. His nose is already bleeding and he holds his head attempting to cushion the blows that rain in on him from Hassan's boots.

He is pulled up and sat onto the chair he left only moments before. Paul reaches behind him and produces a sack and twine. He puts the sack over Colin's head and slaps him. He turns to Dani smiling.

"I said you can go. I believe you, Dani."

John gives Dani a long look before scurrying out of the door. Colin is struggling. The sack thickens his voice.

"It weren't me. It was Dani's soldier!"

Paul shakes his head before landing another blow.

"I don't like losing money."

"But he can get it back for you!" Dani says at once.

"Dani!" Trevor puts a little more bass in his voice than before. Now he speaks mildly. "Wait outside."

She backs up reluctantly, walking slowly out. Sonny follows her. He's immediately on the phone, talking quietly. He follows her around the corner once he's hung up.

Dani exhales loudly.

"Fucking hell Son."

He's nodding.

"I know. That was fucking crazy in there."

"How we gonna get Colin out? We can't just leave him."

Sonny looks over at her.

"Why d'you wind Carly up like that!"

She looks down at his boots.

"Sorry, I couldn't help it. I'm gonna fucking have her when this is done. You know she must have fucking followed us home!"

Sonny sighs, shaking his head. He's already beginning to miss Marie.

"Let's just try and work out how the fuck we're gonna save this boy."

Paul is in there punching and kicking at the sack that is Colin. Dani would like to hold her ears. She can take no more when she hears him scream. She runs back inside.

"Wait. Paul, wait!"

"No, Dani, you were right. This little fellah here is a piss-taker. He needs a fucking lesson." He punctuates the sentence with another punch to the sack. "He's lucky I don't let Hass sort him out."

Colin cries out again, his groaning muffled by the sack. Trevor is looking quizzically at Dani, wondering if there's been some change of plan. He'd been sitting comfortably at the table, nonchalantly watching proceedings, before she burst in with a confused Sonny behind her.

"Yeah, I know." Dani advances, taking the sack from Colin's head, "But you're gonna get your money innit." She's removed the sack to make him more human again, although it'll take more than that to stop Paul now his switch has been flicked. Colin's nose is already broken. He also has a nasty swelling developing over his left eye.

"Come on Paul, he's only young. He's probably the family breadwinner ain't he?"

Paul walks towards Colin again. Dani says, "Wait. Hang on, lets see if he can come up with the money first."

Ayrton is fingering his gun, which is still lying on the table. "Why?"

"Because he's just a kid."

"Playing big man games."

"Yeah, but I'm gonna fix that," she says firmly.

"How?"

Trevor's giving her a warning look. She ignores it, turns away from him and goes over to Colin, the sack still in her hand.

"Colin."

"Fuck you!" She can see how he hates her.

"Colin!"

He spits blood and phlegm at her.

"Go and suck your m ..."

Trevor is out of his seat and on Colin before she can stop him. One punch cracks the eye socket. Colin was sobbing quietly, now he is howling again. Dani looks to Sonny for help. She can't do this by herself. Sonny steps forward, answering the silent call.

"Alright, alright, shut up! Silly cunt's gonna wake the whole neighbourhood."

Ayrton snorts, smirking.

"I'd let him do it if I didn't need my money."

He's indicating Trevor who's sat back down, whistling to himself. You don't even have to know him to realise that's not a good sign. Dani is seriously worried about the boy's safety now. She understands he doesn't want to owe her and that he's pissed off that they chose to believe Dani rather than him. She gets he hates her and normally wouldn't bother herself with why. She's racking her brain, trying to find the key – the way in with him. She now knows even if she persuades the Turks to let Colin go, Trevor isn't done with him. She has to get him to give way somehow, concerned at how easy it was for him to pull Dennis and Marvin in so deep, so quickly.

Sonny speaks as she considers the situation. He's asking for a deal whereby the Turks are repaid all their money, including for today, and Dani and the others leave with the bodies – Colin and Dennis.

Ayrton seemed to be on the verge of agreeing, but Paul has other ideas. He wants to keep Colin. Trevor had stopped whistling when Sonny first spoke and is now smiling. Paul understands this to mean that either way, Dani, Sonny and Trevor would leave with what they came for and their reputation intact.

The others start to relax, but Dani knows if they leave without Colin, there's a danger no one will see him again. She knows the Turks sometimes send people on short holidays and is sure that's what Paul has in mind for Colin. He's so greedy, they wouldn't have to ask him twice to bring something back from abroad. He also has nerve, which means Paul could either wait to see if Colin succeeds or give him up to Customs so others can get through. Life sentence – death sentence, same thing in a foreign country where no one speaks your language.

🐾

Dani looks back at Colin. His eye is horribly swollen, as is his nose. His bottom lip is cut and bleeding. His legs are probably bruised from the kicking.

"I wanna talk to him alone."

"If I didn't know better," murmurs Paul, "I'd think something funny's going on here."

"What you talking about, Paul?" Trevor's on a hair trigger. "We ain't got time for your fucking Charlie paranoia today, OK?"

"You fucking watch your mouth when you talk to me."

He walks back over to Colin.

"Tell me why this bothers you so much, Dani."

He slaps Colin on his already broken nose. Colin cries out. His blood is on Dani's overalls.

"He's just a stupid kid." She looks at Paul meaningfully. "He don't know what's coming."

Paul smirks. Can't get anything by her can you?

"No Dani, he's not just a kid. He's trouble. I'll be doing you a favour."

"I understand what you're saying but it don't look good on my record if I lose him."

Paul smirks again.

"Dani." Sonny indicates the door. "Let's have a chat outside."

She follows him out. It's cold outside and lack of sleep is beginning again to gnaw at her. She yawns. Sonny watches her.

"I know why you want to save him, but some people would just rather go down fighting."

"I just can't work out how the fuck to break him."

It's driving her nuts.

"To be honest Dani, even if you get him out of here, Trevor hates him." He lowers his voice. "Something might happen to him anyway."

She nods. No one has ever gotten away with insulting her mum within Trevor's presence and hearing.

"We can't just leave him. They'll send him you know."

"Yeah, but he won't give in."

She sighs.

"Thanks for backing me."

"It's covered."

"One last try."

She grits her teeth before heading back in the room. She crosses it in strides. Crack! She has punched Colin just under the good eye. He cries out as the others watch, startled.

"You fucking got me all wrong, you know that?"

"What!"

He's beginning to look like Dennis.

"Maybe you think I'm some sort of maternal fucking wet nurse or something. You think you can sit there taking the piss, while I sit here begging for your soul, is that it?"

She kicks his leg.

"Where's the fucking money stashed?"

"I spent it."

She steps back, holding out a hand. She keeps her eyes glued to his.

"Give me something to hit him with."

Trevor smiles when Colin's eyes meet his. Paul hands Dani a table leg that's waiting to be assembled. Dennis hobbles unnoticed outside. He's seen enough bats, bars, fists and boots to last him a lifetime.

"See, Colin, I think you want to show these guys you can take a beating. You think that'll make them like ya ..."

She holds the leg like a baseball bat, adjusting her two-handed grip until it feels comfortable.

"... But I ain't so sure. Where's the money?"

He clenches his jaw with hatred. She aims for the middle of his arm. The blow lands hard, making only a thudding noise, but he cries out. Dani takes a deep breath.

'Think I'm the motherly type do ya? Well, this is for your own good."

She swings again, hitting higher on his arm.

"Go on, Dani!"

Hassan beams as he cheers her on. He's impressed.

"When they gonna get their money back?"

"I told you, you fucking bitch! We spent it."

He's breathing heavily. Dani presses.

"And? What you wanna do, twenty questions? OK, no problem."

'Thwack!' Now the blow lands on his shoulder.

"No! No, you fucking bitch!"

He's screaming now. The Turks are laughing. Trevor and Sonny are grim and this time he flinches when she sets herself to swing again. She's aiming for the side of his head.

"I'll get it! I'll get it."

His swollen lip affects his speech as Paul advances on him, smiling appreciatively sideways at Dani.

"They told me you had a way with words."

Ayrton chuckles as Paul bears down on the snivelling Colin.

"How you gonna pay me?"

"Take these."

Colin points his chin towards his diamond chains. Paul reaches around his neck and releases the catch.

"Thank you. What else?"

Colin's crying now.

"Nice watch," Paul says. Colin nods, so it's removed from his wrist. Hassan moves in now and they take his rings.

"What else?"

"I ain't got nothing else. But I can get it."

"How?"

Ayrton hasn't left his seat. He won't get his hands dirty. He only uses his trigger finger.

"I'll rob it."

Paul laughs. "Have you seen the state of you? You can't

even fucking run, you mug."

Dani looks over at Trevor despairingly. She has failed. She'd given Colin the beating in order for him to avoid any punishment the Turks had in mind. Maybe he can get whoever helped him spend the money to help earn it back. Trevor wants her to accept the situation.

"It's time to go."

Dani's thinking fast.

"Paul. Just a couple more minutes guys please?"

"Give it up, Dani."

"Just five minutes alone. That's all I want."

"Fucksakes." Trevor stands. "Two minutes!" He bends down to Colin. "Make sure I don't have to come back in this room."

She waits until the door bangs shut.

"They're gonna do you brov."

His hatred for her shimmers in the space between them.

"I'm tryna fucking help you!"

He's defiant despite the blood, tears and snot.

"I don't need your help. They want me to do stuff for them. I can do it."

She shakes her head.

"You think they're gonna fucking take you in and treat you like their long lost son?"

"They know I can take it now, don't they?"

She closes her eyes.

"Trust me Colin, you don't wanna work for them."

"Don't I?" He glares at her. "They'll keep me. When they see what I can do when I'm the one tying someone else up ..." He looks into her eyes meaningfully, dropping his voice to a whisper " ... They'll wanna keep me."

"For how long?"

He smiles through the pain.

"The next time you see me you'll be asking me to let someone else off. But I'll tell you straight. You'll be wasting your time, just like you are now."

She had crouched down to make eye contact. Now she stands, defeated.

"I'll tell you something else, Dani."

She turns at the door.

"When I join the Turks." He licks the blood at the corner of his mouth, savouring it. "You should make sure you never give your soldiers up. Someone like you can't walk alone."

She turns and leaves.

This is the worst type of loss, the one where you fail to negotiate a successful outcome, you damage your reputation and you gain yourself a grudgeful enemy into the bargain. Her anger is simmering.

Sonny calls her.

"It's time to go."

She nods, saying nothing. Paul is wearing all of Colin's jewellery. It's not how he dresses, so it looks like a sadistic joke. She sees that Dennis is in the truck with Sonny.

They'll return to the yard and burn the overalls and boots. Trevor will take the boys to Casualty and then put poor Dennis on a train with a wad of money. They'll meet at Dani's later. She's quiet, can't get Colin out of her mind. She's angry at him for engineering the whole thing purely so he can join a gang, angry at her own failure to dissuade him.

Trevor and Sonny know what's bothering her so they don't

question her when she asks that Trevor stay behind with her. They change at the yard and go over to Charlie's.

Changing is meticulous as usual. Each of them in turn stands on the tarpaulin in the back of the truck, to strip off the overalls and boots. Dani goes first as she definitely has Colin's blood on her. Once they've all stripped down to the jeans and tops underneath, the tarpaulin is rolled up and put through the wood cutting machine. Once ground down, it is placed with the wood mulch and dumped. They do this as a precaution whenever blood is spilt.

If anyone ever goes back on an agreement it usually means someone's gonna get hurt. If that happens the chances of Dani's, Sonny's or Trevor's name being mentioned during any police investigation suddenly rockets. They'll always deny presence at any such meeting, so there must be no forensic evidence to contradict that.

Sonny calls Sweets from Charlie's yard. Dani doesn't call Susanna because she is not yet in the right frame of mind. She's wired and still agitated about Carly.

She is in the yard smoking when he gets off the phone.

"You wanna speak to your girl? "

He holds out the phone to her.

"Not right now. "

She's left her own phone back at the office. He figures she's still brooding over Colin, so he doesn't push it. He decides not to repeat what Sweets has just told him about Carly turning up at Dani's flat. He leaves her smoking and heads off half an hour before Trevor arrives. He'll talk to her later.

"What's these for?"

Dani's in the truck with Trevor, who is indicating the new set of overalls she's asked him to bring. He knows what. He really means "who".

"Carly."

She looks straight ahead.

"Did you tell Sonny that?"

No answer. Trevor's starting to think he needs to give her another talking to. Her behaviour over this girl is beginning to warm up again. He can see it would be pointless to try that now. Then again – it was a sly move Carly pulled. Trevor had spoken to Whisky when they went outside. Whisky explained Carly had tricked her brother, who in turn had misled them. John was unaware that Carly and Colin had been in contact. Trevor had just nodded. Sometimes an apology is enough, sometimes it isn't.

"Mikey was following Carly," Trevor tells Dani.

"Does he know where she is now?"

He nods.

"Who's with him?"

"He's gone. Darren and Ellis are with her now."

Even better. She breathes in through her nostrils.

"Lift her."

He already has the phone in his hand.

He indicates the living room behind her with his eyes. Dani freezes. She doesn't turn around.

"She's still here?"

"She's been here all day."

The stupid smile is threatening her expression again.

"What's she been doing?"

"I don't fucking know! I got better things to do than watch her all day."

Mikey's wondering what's going on with her. Dani looks down, clearing her throat. She suddenly feels embarrassed at the thought of being with Susanna in front of all these people.

Susanna is watching from a chair in the living room. She'd been speaking to Sophie and Paula when Dani walked in then out of the room. She knows Dani. She understands she can sometimes be very shy around her if others are present. She smiles. Dani is standing with her back to her and she sees her take a deep breath before turning around. Susanna watches as she chews the inside of her cheek.

Dani looks at her sweat top, pulled across Susanna's chest protectively. She can feel Sonny's eyes on her. She shifts her stance so he can't see her expression. She inadvertently finds herself looking directly at Trevor, who's also watching her curiously.

Soon the whole room is watching the two of them, looking from one to the other. Dani is standing awkwardly with one hand in her pocket. With the other she's combing at her eyebrows with her fingers, pulling them the wrong way. It has the effect of partially hiding her face.

Susanna suddenly gets to her feet and walks out of the room, pulling Dani by the arm as she goes. They walk silently towards the bedroom. It is a while before conversations in the living room resume.

As they reach the bedroom door, Susanna stops. There is no one else in the hallway. Dani smiles at her, opening the door to let her in. Once inside the bedroom, Dani has regained her powers of speech.

"You been here all day, Suse?"

"Yeah. Um – I to took the day off. Is that OK?"

Dani's grin is back.

"Kiss me."

"Will you behave yourself?"

"Promise."

"Liar."

"You gonna stay with me tonight?"

They have their arms around each other now.

"I need to get some things."

"Can we get them tomorrow?"

Susanna strokes her cheek.

"You look tired, baby. We can have a bath when these lot go."

They are kissing as she talks softly.

"Hmmmm."

Susanna laughs.

"You're purring again. Stop it, we can't stay in here."

Dani groans.

"Come on then."

She takes Susanna's hand.

"Dani, wait."

"What babe?"

"Are you gonna tell me what that was all about this morning?"

"You gonna tell me about Carly, then?" Dani's voice has a little edge.

"If you want."

"Let's do this later."

"You're not gonna tell me, are you?"

Dani kisses her.

"I need a spliff. Come on."

"Dani …"

"I'll talk to you later babe, come on." She grabs her around the waist again. "We got plenty of time." She kisses her neck.

"Fine."

They head back to the living room.

"So you met the girls."

"I met Paula before, once, years ago."

"Really?"

"Yeah."

"How come?"

"I was probably looking for you!" smiles Susanna.

"Gimme a spliff, Son?" Dani calls over

He throws one already rolled to her.

"What we drinking?"

Susanna raises an eyebrow.

"Under the counter, straight from Dominica."

Trevor holds up a bottle of something lethal-looking with some sort of leaf suspended in the alcohol. There's no label on the bottle. Dani backs off.

"Nope, out of my league."

She sits down next to Susanna.

"You smoking, Suse?"

"No. I'm OK."

"Sorry," she says quietly, "do you want me not to?"

"No babe, it's fine, just relax."

Dani smiles.

"You know everyone here?"

"Mostly. Just relax, I'm fine. Anyway I'm in the middle of girl talk with Paula."

"Oh yeah? What about?"

"She's filling in the gaps for me."

"Like what?"

Paula leans over.

"Mind your own business. Sweets, come here a minute."

Dani grins, moving over to where Sonny is sitting. He has one hanging out of the corner of his mouth and one he's building on his lap.

"Going it a bit ain't you Son?"

"This is for you."

"You just gave me one."

"It's nearly done. Anyway we're celebrating."

"What, that shit today?"

"No, you got your woman back innit?"

Dani looks over at Susanna who's giggling at something. Sophie and Paula are whispering. She looks at Sonny again, smiling shyly.

"Yeah, she's back."

"You know Carly was here?"

"I know. We lifted her."

"Thought so."

"Sorry. I knew you'd try and talk me out of it."

"Might not have."

"Please!"

"Does that mean all the madness is done then?"

"I fucking hope so."

"She's alright innit?" He indicates Susanna.

"You've changed your tune."

"Yeah, well." He struggles to open his eyes and look at her properly. "Sweets reckons she says all the same stuff you do."

"I do."

Someone knocks on the door to her office.

"Oh boy. Look Paula, I'm sorry. I have to go, can I phone you later?"

"Yeah. Of course. I'm sorry. I thought you knew."

"Thanks for calling me."

Rachel Campbell is Trevor's lawyer. She wakes Dani some hours later. She is the type of lawyer who rarely if ever smiles. Her expression suggests she has no capacity to do so.

"Have you eaten?"

In a daze, Dani croaks "No".

Rachel Campbell snaps at the constable.

"Can you arrange for my client to have some food now please ... and let me know why that hasn't already been done?"

Dani sits up, looking around. Memory clicks in, bringing with it a tidal wave of anxiety, crashing in on her, pounding at her head.

A Styrofoam tray arrives with nondescript lumps of food. Dani puts it to one side on the bench next to her.

"Eat it," Rachel orders her, "your interview is going to be long and difficult."

"I ain't gonna say anything."

Dani looks at the food in disgust, but Rachel is uncompromising.

"You'll need to eat before dealing with this. And you may as well get used to it. You're unlikely to get bail."

Dani picks reluctantly at the container while Rachel sits arranging her papers.

"How many witnesses they got?" The food is disgusting.

"They're not willing to disclose that information."

"Am I the only one arrested?"

"As far as I am aware. It would be better for you if it stays that way."

"They took a bag of spliff butts from my house. They're not relevant."

"Maybe not – but they want to know who you associate with."

Dani continues eating the glop. Obviously Rachel's not the type she can ask to do something dodgy. It is a stroke of luck that her phone was left at the office the day before. They would've had a field day with that …

Rachel says sharply, "They say this is the result of a dispute over a girl. Were you alone when you were arrested?"

She nods.

"Good."

Rachel explains the law to her – what needs to be proven. They agree Dani will say nothing during the interview.

"They'll want to speak to the girl."

Dani looks down.

"What will she say?"

"I don't think she'll talk to them."

"Would she speak on your behalf?"

"I don't want her in Court or nothing like that," Dani says defiantly.

"Give me her address. The police will want to speak to her, so we ought to …"

Dani is scratching at the back of her head.

"Don't know it."

Rachel has to look up from writing her notes.

"Excuse me?"

"I don't know where she lives."

"Do you want to tell me why that is?"

"We only just – I mean she was gonna tell me."

"You just met?"

Her eyebrows are up high above the rims of her glasses.

"No, no! We … It's complicated."

"I need to know."

Her voice is impatient.

"We've been on and off for years." Dani shrugs. "We just got back together."

Rachel keeps her thoughts to herself.

"Where was she when the police arrived?"

Dani is beginning to feel the true weight of what's happening. She massages her temple.

"We had an argument in the night and she left me."

Rachel considers whether to ask the reason for the argument. She decides against it.

The interview lasts long enough for the police to use three tapes. Dani refuses to answer questions, counting in her head when it is suggested Susanna is now comforting Carly. They finally take her back to her cell at four in the afternoon.

The interview was difficult enough, but it's afterwards, when Rachel leaves, that mind games begin. They ignore her call on the bell, forgetting to feed her again until much later. The gaoler promises to let her out for a smoke and then reneges on it. He returns later to tell Dani food's been sent in for her but he won't say who it's from or why she can't have it. In the end she stops asking for anything. She should know better anyway.

Trevor is in the front office of the police station. He's brought another "complete meal in a tin" type of drink. As it's sealed, they've assured him Dani will be allowed to have it. He's told Rachel is on her way back, so he decides to wait. He calls Sonny.

"… Yeah, I'm there now. Rachel's coming back, so they must be gonna charge her … Yeah, Ellis is looking for them now … She's here. I'll call you back."

He stands to shake Rachel's hand.

"Trevor. How are you?"

"Yeah, good. Yourself?"

"Fine. Dani has given me permission to discuss the case with you. Is there any chance you know where her girlfriend lives?"

"I could probably find out."

"Good. I'll call you when I get out."

"How's it looking?"

"I imagine they'll charge and keep her in custody to go to court in the morning."

He shakes his head. Sonny will probably blame him for agreeing to take her to lift Carly.

"Can you check she got the food I sent in, please?"

He says goodbye to Rachel and leaves, fishing his phone out of his pocket again.

It is 11.25 p.m. when he gets the call to say Dani will be in court the next morning. She has also asked that Trevor retrieve her car keys from inside the key cupboard, so he can move her car. He leaves home immediately when he gets that message. There's something naughty in that cupboard, otherwise she'd have asked Sonny who also has keys to her flat.

Dani's flat is a fucking mess. He walks in and has a look around before checking the key cupboard. He does a quick tidy up. She'd hate to see it like this.

Inside the cupboard is a semi-automatic handgun. He releases the magazine housed in the handle. Fuckin' 'ell! It was actually loaded! Where the fuck did she get this? He'll have to hide it. She must have borrowed it from someone. Who the fuck would give her that? Whoever it is had better see him coming first! He wraps the gun in tea towels and puts it at the bottom of a sports bag. He also puts a suit, shirts, underwear and a pair of her shoes in, before leaving.

Dani has asked Trevor to make sure Susanna is not at court, so Paula is trying unsuccessfully to persuade her to stay away. Susanna's angry.

"No! How would you feel if it was Trevor? *You'd* want to be there, wouldn't you? Well then …"

She ends the call.

It's not the first time Dani has been in a police station overnight, but still she feels raw and vulnerable. Her clothes are crumpled and her back is stiff from sleeping on the slab of concrete that's been her bed for the night. She'd refused to use the mattress used by so many other miserable angry detainees.

She sits up stiffly. Her head is pounding again. She shivers, rubbing at the arms of her crumpled sweat top. She must smell awful. There is fluff from the blanket in her hair. Her stomach is grumbling so there's no choice but to eat the dog food placed in front of her. They won't let her have the clothes Trevor's brought, but that's OK because now at least she knows the weapon is sorted.

Rachel has warned she is unlikely to get bail from court.

She'll go to prison today, for the first time in her life. She's asked that her family members are not informed until it's certain bail is refused. She's also asked that Susanna be kept away from the court at all costs. She's afraid of how she'll feel if she has to look Susanna in the eye when she's taken down. She's trying to prepare herself. Her fear is that Carly will only withdraw her statement at the last minute, meaning she could be inside for some time.

They come for her at nine. She is handcuffed again. She has always told the soldiers: "See these wrists. Handcuff no fit dem!" They do now. In truth, if she could go through this completely alone, she'd prefer it. She doesn't want anyone to see her like this.

The journey is tortuous. On many occasions she's looked up at the blacked out windows of prison vans and punched her fist to the left side of her chest in support. Now she can see how many people don't actually notice the vehicle next to them in the traffic. How can they not know that inside, people's lives are falling apart?

At court, she's put in a holding cell. She knows two women from the gay scene.

"Raas Dani! What you doing here?"

Janet's from Leicester or somewhere like that. She's into organised shoplifting, stuff that ends up on market stalls. Dani has held on to stock for her in the past.

"Fucking 'ell!" Sandra, her sidekick and permanent partner in crime, is serious. "Dani, what the fuck have you done?"

"Long story."

"It'd have to be. You got a good brief?"

"Course she has," Janet says. "Got any smokes?"

"Yeah, you want one?"

"Listen we'll twos one, but don't go offering them around unless you know you're getting out."

She gives them one, thinking she'll have to ask Rachel to get her some more.

"Give us one babe?" A skinny junkie is getting up.

"Fuck off."

"What you goin' on like that for? You don't need to fuck me off like that you know. I just ..."

Dani moves over to her quietly and slowly. She whispers into her ear.

"Listen darling. I'm not in the best mood right now. So you need to stop right there, understand?"

The skinny woman looks at Dani with disdain. She's taken so many beatings in her life that threatening her is a complete waste of time. She sneers, "You fucking think you're better than the rest of us. We'll see when you come back down."

She keeps it up until Dani is called up to court. Thankfully, she's first on the list.

She's led up narrow stairs at Highgate Magistrates Court. She stands in between two dock officers and glances over to the public gallery. She can see how bad she must look because of the way they're looking at her. Sonny winks. He can't hide it though. He looks like he wants to cry. Fucking hell, Sweets is with him. They must have got a sitter. She looks grim. She keeps her hand on his arm, supporting him, holding him up. Trevor, Derek and Ellis are also there, sitting apart from the others. They're all business, listening to the case, picking up all the info they can.

Dani looks to Sonny's left. Fuck. Susanna's eyes are wide. Frightened. She has a cap on. It belongs to Dani, though she never wears it. Susanna has her hair in a ponytail and is wearing jeans and a bomber jacket. They stare at each other. Dani watches her reaction when the charges are read out. She looks afraid.

Dani is told to sit down. She looks at the floor, knowing what's coming.

The prosecutor says Carly is vulnerable and has had to leave her home address. It's doubtful whether she'll regain full use of her hand. He describes how the injury was inflicted, maliciously and with deliberate intent. He says bail should be denied because of the substantial sentence that will be imposed if Dani is convicted. Her barrister offers a surety of ten thousand pounds, but that only seems to antagonise the bench even more. They ask questions about where that money is coming from. They make assumptions about her ability to raise large sums of money. Bail is refused.

18

Letters

Mr. Ian McHale,
18 Wicklow Avenue,
Crouch End,
N8 3PB.

Dani Fenton,
Prison Number MW1514,
HMP Bronzefield

Son,

I always go on about telling the truth, so here's a couple for you:

1. I didn't tell you about the lift, because you're too good for stuff like that. You never want to do those things because you're better than that.
2. You're what I've been trying all my life to be.
3. You were that before you knew me.
4. Make sure you chase up Curtis in Bristol. He's gonna be good. You'll see.
5. Please try to send my stuff in before Thursday so I

can get my canteen on a Monday.

6. I'm up in the Crown court in a month (November 10th), so you can come then.

7. I only want Trevor visiting me until then. I know you understand.

Love to Sweets and the baby sweets.

Dani.

P.S. Please get this letter to Susanna for me. I know you won't read it.

Susanna,

I'm sorry about how I acted on the visit. Obviously you know there was a bit of an incident after you left, so I hope you can understand that I don't want you visiting me again. I would only be watching everyone else.

I'm sorry that the drawer is empty, so now you have nothing to look back on.

I've got about a thousand sorries and even more promises. Hopefully I will get a chance to give them to you soon.

I know you heard what the damage was likely to be. I'm hoping you delay the decision on junior until you know for definite. You know I'll understand if you have to go ahead. You also know when I'm done paying, I'll walk into your nice, quiet Mr. and Mrs. house and walk you straight out.

I'll see you then.

Dani.

Mr. Ian McHale,
18 Wicklow Avenue,
Crouch End,
N8 3PB.

Dani Fenton,
Prison Number MW1514,
HMP Bronzefield.

This one's for you, Son,

Thanks for the parcel, I got it before Monday.

I hear Curtis is on board. Well done.

Tell Trevor I'm sending him a V.O. for next week. I had to send some to the fam. My mum has flipped out. My dad's just going on about how he knew it would happen sooner or later. To tell the truth he's probably right.

Do me a favour. Stop giving me the pity looks when you see me at court. I'm OK.

My brief says I can't get bail now unless something changes, so I'll see you in May.

Love to Sweets and the baby sweets.

P.S. Make sure my brief gets the stuff back that the police don't want and give it to Suse.

This one's for Suse

It's good to get your letters. I know where I'm at then. I like that you are living at my place, but it feels strange to think of you there when I'm not. I'm glad your job is going well, you should stop taking time off. Anyway I won't be in court for a while now. I'm trying to get the stuff back for the drawer.

I can't say what I want to say but you know anyway.

I think maybe if you dressed really badly, it would be OK you coming on a visit. I'll send you the next V.O. Don't come with Trevor.

Dani.

Dani's hair has grown. She has twisted it into short locks. She has gained weight from all the stodge and weight training. It's her antidote to sexual frustration.

She is already seated when Susanna walks in, wearing jeans and a quilted jacket, which is zipped right up to the collar. Dani watches hungrily as she crosses the floor to her table. They kiss until Dani blushes. She smiles.

"Thanks for the radio."

"Are you OK?" Susanna wants to hold her.

"Yeah yeah I'm alright. What about you?"

"Well I miss you and I'm sleeping in your bed alone. I got Sophie to stay the other night."

They stare at each other for a while …

"You might be a bit heavy for me now, babe," Susanna jokes.

Dani smiles.

"Fuck all else to do."

"Can't you do education?"

"Not till I'm convicted."

Susanna looks down at the table. Dani could kick herself for saying that.

"Trevor asked me if I wanted him to sort it out," Dani says thoughtfully.

"What did you say?"

"I told him no."

"Why?"

"It's my own fault I'm here. After the club, I should've expected Carly to do some shit. Instead of just telling her why I did it, I went and taunted her. Do you think it's true about her not being able to use her hand?"

"It might be."

"Fuck. And now I'm away from you and even if she doesn't get on the stand she can just wait it out till May. I deserve it. I done everything I been telling my boys not to do."

They are silent for a while, then Dani adds, "I want Trev to sort it but I feel like if he does, things are only gonna get worse. Anyway I don't really think she's gonna go all the way with this."

"What if she does, Dani? What if she actually goes to court and gives evidence?"

"Rachel reckons three ... Don't Suse."

"I'm sorry. I just ..." She swallows.

"I meant what I said. If that happens you go do what you have to. I'll come and get you."

"Dani, how can I do that? I can't have our baby with you here."

Dani says nothing. She's twisting her hair. Susanna feels bad for stressing her out.

"It's OK, Dan. We'll work it out."

They're both silent again. Susanna looks round the room. It's full of people like her, trying to make the inmates forget where they are. She tries to smile.

"I like your new physique, actually."

Dani doesn't smile.
"Does anyone know where she is?"
"Carly?"
"Yeah."
"I saw her last week at Venus."
"What the fuck were you doing there?"
She apologises when Susanna glares at her.
"I was meeting Sonny there to talk about you."
"I'm sorry. I'm sorry."
She's barely holding it together.
"Will you send me another Visiting Order?"
No answer.
"OK. Whatever you need, it's OK." She speaks soothingly again, echoing the other visitors. Dani is not listening anyway. She growls, "Did you talk to her?"
"We don't need to go through all that now."
"What?"
Dani's getting angry.
"Look, I can't explain it," Susanna says quickly.
"Try."
"Dani …"
Susanna watches helplessly as Dani stands up suddenly, trying to lift the table off the floor. But it's screwed into the floor, as are the chairs. She kicks at the table violently before storming out of the visits hall. Susanna is still crying when she gets back to the car where Sophie is waiting in the driver's seat.

Mr. Ian McHale,
18 Wicklow Avenue,
Crouch End,
N8 3PB.

Dani Fenton,
Prison Number MW1514,
HMP Bronzefield.

This one's for you, Son,

More truths.

The intention was never to have the boys doing extra work for us. That's not why we got them in the first place is it?

If I didn't have them I would have had to make peace over what I took from the club that night.

I still have no answer for Trevor. It depends on what day you ask me. I'm trying to stick to no.

🐾

This one's for Suse.

Another sorry, to add to your collection.

I don't know if you're still at my place. I hope so.

Last night I counted to 700 and it still didn't feel better. I need to get out of here. I'm not freaking out and I'm not sending a message. I just needed to tell you.

I've got a new trick. I give myself advice as if I'm one of my boys. That way, when I get out I'll make sure not to do anything stupid. Any one of the things I want to do would put me straight back in here. I used to think I would never be that stupid. Now I know I am.

Please come again. I promise I'll be good.

Dani.

It's a Saturday morning in February when Susanna walks across the visits hall, her expression grim. As usual she turns a few heads, so Dani's jaw is already working overtime by the time she sits down. Then she sees Susanna's face.

"What's wrong, Suse?"

"You mean apart from the obvious?"

Dani sits back in her chair.

"Are you alright?"

"No. I want a baby."

Silence.

"Well, who do you want me to tell?" Susanna asks.

Dani is twisting at her hair again. She looks up at Susanna darkly.

"Is this the bit when I'm supposed to say 'OK Suse, go get pregnant?"

Susanna draws herself up in her chair.

"Do I look like I'm asking for your fucking permission?"

Dani grits her teeth.

"Why don't you say what you came here to say, Suse. Come on! Let's get it over with."

She glares across the table.

"Don't take that attitude with me Dani! I didn't travel all this way to take your shit OK! I wanna say 'what the fuck were you thinking?" She's mimicking Dani's voice. "I wanna say I shouldn't be living alone in your fucking flat, that your fucking ego is the reason you're sat there, looking daggers at me. That I shouldn't have to have people banging on the door and shouting things about you all through the night when I have to work the next day."

She sits back, breathing heavily.

A few heads have turned in their direction while they sit silent for a while. Then Susanna lets out a huge sigh.

"I'm sorry."

Dani's too afraid to ask if it's the time of the month.

"It's OK."

"I am. I'm sorry."

She reaches across the table, taking Dani's hand.

"I miss you too." Dani smiles.

"You're not angry at me?" She strokes Dani's fingers.

"No. You're right. But I don't want you to get pregnant."

"I know."

They sit staring at each other. Dani winces. The pain of not being able to hold her is almost physical. She is gripping her hand so tightly that Susanna has to pull away.

Dani swallows.

"Suse, I –"

"Dani, if you *ever* do anything like this again, I'm gone." She gets up. "And this time I won't fucking come back."

She turns and leaves, her expression more grim than when she arrived.

Dani sighs. Not all the visits are bad like this. Sometimes Susanna tells her over and over again how much she loves and misses her. Sometimes they talk about their past. When Susanna gets angry (which happens a lot lately) Dani just tells herself she deserves it, holding onto her for as long as she can.

Susanna arrives home tired, hungry and irritable. Sophie

has dropped her off and she is walking with her head down towards the block. Now she stands in the lift, shaking her head angrily as it grates and groans its way up to the third floor. The door slides open, banging at the frame.

"How's your lover girl?"

Carly is waiting on the landing. Susanna is too worked up to do what she ought to which is step back into the lift and call the police.

"You need to get away from here."

"Oh do I?" Carly takes a step towards her. "And why's that then?" She smiles nastily. "Is your hero gonna come and rescue you?"

Susanna closes her tired eyes.

"Carly, please just go away."

"Let me come inside. We need to talk."

"No! I mean it Carly. I want you to go."

Carly takes hold of her arm with her good hand.

"Susanna, you don't just walk out on me like that and that's it! We have to talk."

"About what? I told you ..."

She pulls her arm away angrily as Carly blocks her path.

"What did you tell me? That you wanna be with her? Well, she's gone now. She ain't coming back for years, so you need to think about it."

Susanna turns away.

"There's nothing to think about."

"What do you mean, nothing?" Carly's raising her voice. "You thought you could just use me to get her jealous and then dash me to one side, but it backfired didn't it?"

Susanna lowers her voice, ashamed.

"That's not what happened."

"So what happened Sue? What happened to 'We'll settle

down and we'll have a baby?'"

"I said I'd think about it. You only knew I wanted children because I told you that as a friend. I didn't think you'd be using it to try and trap me!"

"Trap you!" She rams the arm in a sling up against Susanna's throat. "Trap you! You fucking bitch. If it weren't for me, they'd be taking turns on you down the nearest crack house!"

Susanna cracks her hand hard across Carly's jaw.

"Get away from me!"

Carly's fist slams into the side of her face.

"Make me." She shoves the arm harder, pressing Susanna against the wall. "You didn't know it was healing, did ya?" She indicates her hand. "I ain't telling the old bill that though. They still think I can't do nothing with it." She sneers. "The longer I keep saying I can't use it, the more years your precious Dani's gonna get. And trust me, if you don't give me the chance that I deserve, I'm gonna make both of your lives a fucking misery."

Susanna is glaring at her, the tears running down her face. She's wondering whether to kick or go for the bad hand, when they hear shouting coming from behind one of the doors on the landing.

"I've called the police!"

Carly falters. Susanna gasps through gritted teeth.

"I said, get away from me!"

Carly grimaces, finally stepping back.

"By the time she gets out you'll be back on the drugs again. Then she won't want you anyway."

She walks to the door at the opposite side of the landing and jumps down the stairs, taking them two at a time. Susanna holds herself together until her shaking hand manages to guide the key correctly into the lock. Her cheek is bruised.

She sinks down onto the floor once the front door is closed.
She presses the heels of her hands into her eyes and sobs.

19

Trust

It's early April and Dani has a date at court. She hasn't bothered to mention it to anyone because it's only a brief hearing to extend the time she is to be held in custody. She has no wish to disrupt everyone's day. Rachel has told her they won't oppose the application. She could have agreed to waive her own attendance at the hearing, but Rachel thinks it wise to use the opportunity and go through more of the evidence with her, so Dani gets a day out.

Who would have thought being handcuffed and made to sit in a vehicle for over two hours could be the highlight of someone's week? The metal cubicle in the prison van is barely big enough to accommodate a human being, but still it's a change of scenery. Her cellmate's been driving her nuts with constant whining about her boyfriend.

When Dani gets to court, Rachel tells her Carly has made a further, more damning statement. It now appears Carly is actually going to give evidence in court against her. She's really going for it. Dani sighs heavily.

Not for one moment had she believed Carly would ever really do this. It's just not what people like them do. Dani had always believed herself too smart, too well connected ever to be in this situation and she'd kept herself strong by taking her rightful punishment without complaint.

She figured the case would get dropped when after having made her point, Carly would fail to appear on the day of trial and then they'd all move on. She knows what she did was wrong and Carly knows Susanna's off limits. That's fair, isn't it? What more does she fucking want!

Rachel Campbell stands up before the prosecutor has a chance to speak. She's so eager she's failed to notice Dani hasn't yet been brought up to court. She's like a rabid dog with a bone and there is no way she's going easy on this prosecutor, trainee or not.

"Your Honour, there is a matter I wish to raise."

The Judge doesn't bother looking up from his papers, letting out a weary, "Yeeesss."

This woman is the bane of his life. She'll nitpick every single point of law and procedure until the whole court room, he, the jury, the prosecutor, even her own client sometimes, gives in and concedes. He suppresses a yawn. If he tries to curtail her she'll merely mount argument on top of argument until no one can remember the salient issue.

"Thank you, your Honour. You see I was served with additional evidence from the complainant, Carly Bennett, moments before your Honour came into court. It was my intention to go through this evidence with my client at the conclusion of this hearing, but it has come to my notice that within this additional statement, the complainant refers to an incident, whereby she herself has been arrested for assaulting and harassing the very woman she alleges is the reason my client attacked her."

The prosecutor stands and objects but she continues to talk over him, flashing him a withering look over her spectacles.

"The prosecution case is that Bennett and the woman in question, Susanna Grange, are in a committed relationship and my client threatened and attacked Bennett out of jealousy and terrorised Ms. Grange, despite the fact Ms. Grange apparently has no wish to be in a relationship with my client."

Rachel's tone becomes more forceful.

"Yet in this more recent statement, Bennett admits Ms Grange is in fact living at my client's address and visiting her in custody regularly. More tellingly, your Honour, she admits assaulting Ms Grange because of her continued relationship with my client. Your Honour, Bennett was arrested outside my client's address as a result of a member of the public raising the alarm."

The prosecutor finally finds his voice.

"Your Honour, whilst the Crown concedes these admissions were made as a result of Ms Bennett's arrest, Ms Bennett also states the situation arose from a misunderstanding, brought about by her worry for Ms. Grange's safety around the defendant. There is ample medical evidence to support the original allegation for which the defendant Fenton is to stand trial. Moreover, the matters surrounding the arrest of Ms Bennett can be put before the jury at trial."

Rachel stands again, the bit between her teeth.

"In my submission, your Honour, the credibility of the witness Bennett has been fatally damaged by these admissions and ..."

Dani lies back in the cell blowing smoke up to the ceiling as she mulls it all over. She's wondering how she will break the news to Susanna, who has been sullen on her recent visits. Dani's been worried this behaviour may be the prelude to a relapse. She can't let this latest development be the thing that tips the balance. She's gonna have to call in Trevor. Contrary to what most people believe, she is reluctant to do this. Every time he has to do something for her, Sonny or one of the soldiers, it's a risk because he goes all out. Trevor doesn't do half measures.

Rachel has brought tobacco to court for her and she's spent the entire morning puffing away as if Christmas has come. It's funny the way your priorities get screwed when you're inside. When they tell her that her hearing is next, she makes them wait, dragging her heels so she can have a few extra puffs. She's in no hurry to sit yawning at some prosecutor's droning voice. She'll be like royalty when she gets back to the prison, everyone's best friend.

When she is finally led into court, the hearing is well under way. The judge doesn't even notice her arrival because of the heated argument going on between prosecution and defence …

Barbs are flying back and forth across the courtroom as the prosecutor mounts a desperate fight to save a case he was only handed this morning by a colleague. There is no way he can return to the police and tell them that it was thrown out at what should have been a routine hearing. The judge too is angry and wants the officer in charge of the case to attend in the afternoon to provide further information.

He adjourns proceedings until 2 p.m.

Rachel attends the cells, her expression as always giving nothing away.

"We'll just have to see what the judge decides."

She peers over her glasses at Dani, who is not even listening, as she bangs on the glass at one of the screws passing by.

"Oi! Give us a light, Guv."

Rachel looks skyward. She cannot tell if Dani fully understands the significance of this morning's proceedings.

"Do you want to go through this now?"

She is holding Carly's statement up vertically. Dani shakes her head, her brow low over squinting eyes, until she sees the writing on the back. Her eyes flicker as she just manages to suppress the sudden jolt within. Rachel stands, gathering the papers.

"I'll see you up in court."

"Sorry. Wait. Let me just read it before we go up."

Rachel hesitates.

"This is the only copy. I've borrowed it from the prosecutor. I'll get them to run one off for you."

Dani is holding herself in.

"No! I might as well look at it now. That's why I'm here innit?"

She smiles suddenly. "I'll give it straight back to you in court."

"Any reason for the sudden interest?"

Dani meets her gaze silently. The way to keep a good lawyer is to only ever answer the questions they ask you, and sometimes not even those.

Rachel considers her. Well that's what you want, a fully engaged client rather than a preoccupied one. She hands the statement over to a salivating Dani.

"I'll see you up there."

The afternoon hearing has Dani's full attention.

"Your Honour, the complainant has confirmed her wish to pursue this case. In those circumstances, the prosecution feels it is appropriate to continue the case against Ms. Fenton, notwithstanding recent events."

Dani is confused. What recent events? She hasn't bothered to read the statement, as she was only interested in the information on the reverse side of the page. Whatever the fuck they're on about, she has to get this case dropped.

The two Danis are at war. One argues this can't go on forever. She'll get home eventually. The other counters that if Carly goes missing now, the case against her will collapse now. She's been going back and forwards over the same internal dispute since her incarceration, but today has made her mind up. She can't face telling Susanna that Carly is intent on getting her put away. She knows Susanna is seconds away from disappearing. Whenever she does that, there's never any guarantee Dani will see her again. No. Carly is forcing Dani to up the ante. She'll be using her phone call tonight to contact Trevor.

Rachel is on her feet, arguing the original reasons for withholding bail cannot be valid in the present circumstances. The judge agrees. Dani is granted bail on condition she stays away from Carly. She sits stunned in the courtroom. She can't take in what Rachel hurriedly tells her after the hearing.

She assures Dani she'll contact her by letter, explaining everything.

"What just happened?

The dock officer explains if her paperwork can be done in time, she can be released from court without the need to return to the prison.

"Your brief doesn't want to see you in the cells cos that will slow down your processing."

Dani grins.

"Did I just fucking get bail?"

The screw laughs.

"That's what the paperwork says."

Dani laughs loud.

"Why?"

"I didn't hear it all. I was trying to get you up to court remember?"

A male dock officer walks past.

"Something about someone harassing the witness."

Dani knits her brow.

"That wouldn't make them let me out, would it?"

The man shrugs, continuing down the hall. His colleague picks up the phone to get the relevant clearance.

"Maybe one witness did something to the other witness?"

Dani flicks a hand nonchalantly.

"No, she wouldn't do that." She shakes her head confidently. "She wouldn't try that shit with me."

"Sorry, mate." Another of the female officers interrupts. "We've got to take you back to the prison. But don't worry, you'll be out tonight."

Three agonising hours pass before she is finally escorted from the wing. She doesn't remember there being so many sliding glass doors on her arrival. She must have been in shock. Finally she steps up to the little door cut out of the huge one, clutching a large plastic bag containing her belongings. HM PRISON SERVICE is emblazoned on it, luridly. She's been given a travel warrant, a piece of paper allowing her free travel home. She takes a bus for the final leg of the journey. Even though she's in a hurry, the idea of going on the underground is unpalatable. She could have called Trevor or Sonny or any of the boys but she's on a mission.

"On a Mish" they used to say when they were younger. That usually meant either looking for weed to buy or customers to sell it to. Today it has an entirely different meaning. They'd think she'd lost her mind if they knew she'd allowed herself to be seen in public with her clothes in a prison bag. An old black lady looks hard at her, shaking her head disapprovingly. Dani doesn't even notice.

She's not ready to see Susanna yet. First she's gotta get this fucking case chucked. She knows she could call Trevor but instead goes straight to Charlie's. She's gonna sort this out her way. She'll only threaten her this time. There's no need for any more violence, but Carly is taking the piss! She heads around the back.

The door from the kitchen is always open. Charlie jumps to his feet when a prison bag comes sailing over the garden wall. Dani is now clambering over after it. As Charlie sees her, he grins.

"Shit! You nearly gave me a fucking heart attack! Come here, man!" He wraps his huge frame around her, squeezing hard. "When did you get out?"

When he releases her, she isn't smiling. Why isn't she happy?

"What's going on, Dani?"

She scratches distractedly at her unkempt hair.

"I need a car."

Charlie frowns.

"What for? Where's Sonny and Trevor?"

"They don't know I'm out yet." She finally meets his gaze.

Charlie puts a hand gently on her elbow.

"Hey. What you doing man?"

As he bends to look properly into her face, she turns away.

"You gonna help me or not?"

"Yeah. Yeah." He's watching her closely. "Why you dressed like that in broad daylight, Dani?"

She's wearing a black jogging suit with black sneakers. Charlie is one of the few people who know the significance of that.

"It's what I put on when they arrested me, Charlie, alright? Now are we done with the twenty questions?"

She's winding herself up for the job, getting agitated. He nods slowly.

"Come in and have something to eat first. Then you can have the car."

She shakes her head.

"You must be hungry, Dani. Just come in. You can go straight up to the flat."

Again she shakes her head.

"I need them car keys, Charlie."

He holds up a hand.

"Let me make you a burger or something, or just some chips. It won't take long."

He's not going to help her unless she agrees.

"Yeah, alright."

She sits down in the chair he had previously occupied. When he comes back out to the garden she's gone and the toolbox inside his shed has been ransacked.

20

Treasure

"The devil makes work for idle hands" her mum used to say but to Dani he has far more fertile ground in the whirring of an overwrought mind.

Her breathing is laboured as she trawls the back streets in search of a car. Her anger is smouldering, her thoughts savage. "I only just got her back and this cunt is tryna make her leave me. She don't care about My Suse. Anyone can see how stressed out Suse is but you'd rather hurt me even if it means her going off on a bender again."

She's muttering furiously to herself now. "Yeah well you're gonna get the fright of your fucking life tonight. You're lucky I don't fucking cave your head in for ya. It's only cos of My Suse why I don't fucking knock you to fuck!"

She avoids the eyes of passing shoppers, feeling that maybe their looks are more than normal glances. With the anger building comes the paranoia that others can sense she's up to no good. She needs to cut her hair. It's making her look wild.

The problem with her talent for seeing and sensing all

that she can see when she stares and scrutinises is she has no idea how much others can see and sense when they look back at her. What she does is easy, effortless skill to her. How can others then fail to see she's so close to being in the grip of that white-hot rage blowing her gaskets and tripping all her circuits?

She finds a car.

Charlie has called Sonny. He in turn has contacted Trevor who is now barking orders down the phone. They call around the various sites the soldiers are working on, and tell them to leave it and start looking.

Sonny is already massaging the back of his own neck.

"You should call Whisky. Just ask him straight where Carly's address is, Trev. It's obvious, innit? Where else is she going?"

"He ain't gonna tell us that, Son."

"Well he'd better! Cos if Dani gets there before we do …"

Trevor shakes his head wearily.

"I can't take the chance John won't just call the police on her. She'd be back inside before the morning. Fuck!" He bangs his forehead with the heel of his hand. "And if that happens, Carly might take the chance and go to court. They'd have Dani stitched up good and proper then, wouldn't they?"

Sonny is looking out on the yard as if she'll suddenly materialise in front of him.

"You know, she might just go straight to Susanna."

Trevor shakes his head.

"No. She's flipped out. If she was going home she'd have got us to pick her up."

"Yeah." He's right. "Shall I call her though, Susanna?"

"No. Leave her out of it for now. She'll freak out cos she'll know what Dani's doing ... Hold on."

Rachel is returning his call. He tells her Dani's sleeping and that she was unclear about what happened in court.

"... It all happened so fast you know."

"Trevor. I've already sent a letter to her. It sets everything out she needs to know."

"Yeah, yeah. Sure." Trevor has his genial voice on. "Cos she's like a little sister, you know what I mean? When I'm lecturing her I just wanna make sure I know what I'm on about."

His face is ashen by the time he ends the call. He makes another quickly.

"I need that address now. It's urgent, mate."

She only recognises one of the barbers at Finsbury Park. The rest either ignore her, or give her hostile looks to which she is impervious.

The young guy cutting her hair is enjoying himself. He kicks her chair, drawing the clippers along the side of her head, as it spins. He moves with flourishes, drawing the clippers in quick, upward movements. She'd had her doubts when he started, cutting roughly at her mini locks. She watches with grim satisfaction as the months of containment are shorn from her head, falling lifeless to the floor. She stares up at herself in the mirror, pulling in air through her nostrils.

"Yeeeaah."

Dani stands, her hair completed. She looks like her old self again. She smoothes the tapered hair at her neck, imagining Susanna stroking her there before pushing the thought from her mind.

There's one place she has to go. One person she has to see

before she does it.

Sonny is on the phone to Sweets.

"If she turns up, don't let her leave, OK? Don't try and call me cos she'll bolt. I'll check in with you. If she's there you say we need nappies, alright?"

"Alright. How comes she got out, babe?"

"I can't talk now Sweets."

She can hear the panic in his voice.

"OK. Sonny, don't worry. Everything will be fine."

Neither of them believes that.

Dani parks the rickety old Ford Fiesta around the corner. Whoever owns it will be ecstatic it's been stolen because it's just about ready for the scrap yard. They'll do much better off the insurance. She knows this for a fact because she's torched cars in the past for the odd fifty quid. She'd make more on it by getting Trevor to help her remove any useful parts, which they'd then sell as scrap before lighting it up. Life was much simpler then.

The bell above the shop door rings as she enters.

"Mr. Goldenberg. It's Dani," she calls out.

She says it loud so she doesn't startle him walking up behind.

"No need to shout." He chuckles. "You will still be Dani even if you whisper."

He is sitting hunched in front of a tailor's dummy, snipping surplus threads from a shirt.

She smiles, lopsided.

"Why do you sit with your back to the door? This is Hackney, you know."

"At my age," he says, "whoever chooses to come through that door is welcome."

She shakes her head.

"I know you heard the bell. Why didn't you turn around? I could be anybody."

"No. Not anybody." He finally turns, smiling up at her. "Somebody."

She rolls her eyes. Still, she is smiling.

He takes in her outfit.

"This I did not make for you."

She laughs.

"What will it be today Dani, pink?"

She grins.

"Or maybe sky blue?"

She'd tell him what a piss-taker he is, only she never swears in front of Mr. Goldenberg.

"Next time." She points up at a roll of black material. "How about that one today?"

He sighs theatrically, standing and taking up his tape measure.

"Tell me everything she said Charlie. Word for word."

Trevor is pacing the garden. He couldn't just sit and wait. He had to do something.

"She didn't say anything, man."

"She must have fucking said something!"

Charlie tells him all he can remember. He never enjoys being around Trevor when he's like this, particularly as Sonny isn't with him. Trevor goes to the shed.

"And you don't know what's missing?"

He shakes his head.

"I never use that stuff. My cousin Vass does all the repairs."

"Did you have a hammer?"

"Think so. Yeah, there would have been."

"Chisel?"

He shrugs apologetically.

"I dunno, mate."

"What about knives?"

"Yeah. There should definitely be a Stanley knife in there cos Vass was stripping wires a week or two ago."

Trevor closes his eyes momentarily. He points inside.

"Are all your kitchen knives in there Charlie?"

"Yeah. She never came inside."

"Check again."

She is standing as the old tailor measures her sleeves.

"You have been away?" he asks, looking at her closely.

Her look gives him the answer. He nods.

"How are your parents?"

She makes a face, swaying a hand from side to side. He moves around her, pulling his tape measure across her back to measure the width of her shoulders.

"All children have to go their own way, but still there are many ways to make their parents proud, no?"

She is thinking about that one.

"You still have the gardening business?"

"Yeah."

"And Sonny is your right-hand man?"

"Yeah, as always," she says.

"Yes. Yes." She knows he's nodding, that way he does.

"These are your treasures in life, Dani. Friends you can trust and parents who stand by you." He shrugs, "Sometimes you have to fight to protect your treasures, no?"

"Yeah." Dani nods slowly.

He moves around to face her again, measuring from her neck to the top of her thigh.

"But Dani, you must always take care not to lose many treasures while focusing upon only one."

She swallows, looking down at the black sneakers on her feet. It usually takes longer to mull over the things he tells her. There are some times when his words are enough to help her change course. This is not one of those times.

His eyes flicker to hers.

"Give me two weeks." He indicates the material.

She shakes his hand.

"Thanks, Mr. Goldenberg. Take care of yourself."

He nods, lifting a finger as he turns away.

"Try to do the same."

21

The Skids

Susanna walks onto the estate looking all about her. The late nights and early starts are relentlessly sapping at her strength. Her resolve is weakening by the day. Each morning she has to turn up at work on time and looking alert. Now that she has managed to get this job in advertising, she has to be creative, patient and flexible, all with a smile on her face, to prove they were right to take the chance on her. Every day she has to remind them how talented she is in preparation for the inevitable.

In the past, whenever she has returned from her relapse and disappearance, she's been forced to start again at the beginning, at the bottom. This time she is determined not to burn this bridge, because it is such a good job. She has the ability and she could do so well here, but every day is more difficult than the one before.

Each night she has to defend herself against the barrage of threats and abuse, most of which she would probably agree with if her wretched tiredness would allow her to think for even a moment.

She exhales through her nostrils when she closes the

front door behind her, without incident. Now she has taken to checking inside the flat before relinquishing her coat.

It's the skids. That's where she is. Sliding helplessly, hopelessly towards that familiar crash at the bottom. Being swept up in Dani's emotional fire that swirls and leaps up into the sky, always feels like the summit. But the summit has a very small surface area. It's never long before the two of them are skidding separately downwards to where the debris has such a familiarity that it is almost like an old friend. Come, lie down, it says. Come and rest in the place where you can be the real you.

She calls her best friend.

"I'm home, Soph."

"Do you want me to come over?"

"No, no. It's fine."

"I don't mind."

"No, honestly. I'm just going to eat, have a bath and get some sleep."

"Maybe if you take the phone off the hook, you'll – "

"I can't, in case I miss Dani's call. Sometimes she calls early."

Sophie sighs. She wishes her friend had never met that girl.

"Alright. Well, call me if you need me … and make sure you eat."

"OK."

She ends the call. She would love Sophie to come and be with her, just to field the calls, which she can never ignore in case they're from the prison. The problem is, once she's on the skids the first thing she has to do in preparation is start to disconnect. Pushing Sophie away is always a delicate matter because she's alive to Susanna's warning signs. Other people are much easier, except of course, Dani.

She misses her so much. When she's gone, it won't hurt so badly because when the pain starts to nip at her she will act before it really starts to take hold. She can line them up, snort them up and leave the planet.

She shudders. It won't be long now.

🐻

PC Church is on the way home when he gets a call from his superior, DC Cazenove.

"Sorry to do this to you mate, but I need you to stop off at Carly Bennett's house. You know, the witness in the girly wrestling case."

Church laughs.

"I'm sorry but I'm already in Putney, nearly home. What's the urgency?"

"Fuck it. I'll do it myself. I'm leaving in about an hour."

"Sorry about that."

"No. Not your fault, mate. Some rookie prosecutor fucked up today and now the suspect's been granted bail. I'm guessing they never thought to tell the victim, so I thought one of us had better let her know."

"True."

"Don't worry about it. It's all a load of crap anyway. The girly's going back and forwards between the suspect and the victim anyway. With a bit of luck they'll all have run each other through by the morning."

Church chuckles again.

"By the way, the horse came in."

"Did it!" Cazenove's delighted. "How much did we win?"

"Fifty-two quid each."

"Blimey! That wasn't bad for a three pound bet."

"You're buying lunch tomorrow."

"Kentucky it is then."

They're both laughing as the call ends.

Sonny has Darren and Ellis in his office.

"You know when you lifted Carly, did you find out where she lived?"

Both shake their heads.

"You sure?"

"Straight up." Ellis is looking around at all the activity. "We lifted her at Dani's place and we just chucked her out on the road after."

"Alright."

He turns to Trevor.

"What about Dennis? He was looking for her. He might have followed her to Carly's."

Trevor shakes his head.

"I tried him already. He never got nowhere before Colin pulled him in to that truck job." He sighs. "Well, the only thing is Dani probably don't know where Carly lives either. We just have to find her before she tricks it out of someone."

Susanna lies in the bath staring at the phone, which she has pulled out onto the floor in the hallway. Ring. Don't ring.

Will Dani be OK when she stops taking her calls? She'll know straight away. She'll send her friends around but it will be too late. Susanna will have vanished.

It's dark now. Dani has been lying in the reclined seat for an hour, just waiting. Fate, luck … all that stuff can be baffling can't it? She pats the folded statement in her pocket. The adrenaline is hurting her temples.

She sits up, reaching under the seat for the chisel, placing it in one pocket and zipping it up. Now the screwdriver, that goes deep in the trouser pocket with no zip. The Stanley knife is zipped up on the right. The hammer needs to be concealed and muffled when in use. She found a Chamois leather in the boot earlier. Perfect. She wraps it tightly round the head, zips her top up to the neck and shoves the hammer up her sleeve. Then she pulls the drawstring from the hem of the sweat top and winds it around her sleeve, pulling it tight and securing the hammer to the inside of her arm.

Saddle up.

Her mum loves westerns. It's what the cowboys say before they go off to kill the people that need to be killed.

The phone rings by Susanna's bed. She takes a deep breath, picking up the receiver.

"Hello?"

"Hi Susanna, it's Paula."

She exhales.

"Oh hi. How are you?"

Paula looks at Trevor, shaking her head. "She's not there," she mouths. "Yeah I'm fine, Susanna. Just thought I'd see how you are."

"Thanks. I'm OK."

She has deliberately not told any of Dani's friends about Carly. Even if they keep it from Dani, she knows Trevor wouldn't let it go.

"Did you see her on Sunday?"

"Yeah. She's OK – well – not too bad. You know ..."

Her voice trails off and again, Paula shakes her head at Trevor. Dani's definitely not been in contact.

"Yeah I know. And how are you coping? Susanna, you know you can come over any time."

"Thanks, Paula." She looks across at her own reflection in the mirror. "I'm just burying myself in work at the moment."

Paula nods. "That's probably the best way."

"It passes the time."

"Don't worry. She'll be home before you know it."

Trevor shoots her a warning look before slamming the door behind him.

DC Cazenove pulls his squad car up behind a battered old Ford Fiesta. Upstairs in the house, Carly is getting dressed. She's slept most of the day and now she's ready to go out on the prowl. That bitch. What did she call me last night? A wannabe? Bitch. She's about to pick up her keys when there is a knock at the door.

You can climb up balcony by balcony but that's kind of obvious. Someone only has to be closing their curtains in the next block and black suit or not you're lit up like a fucking flare. The drainpipes are always best. These buildings are so old the pointing's usually shot. You can get good footholds in there. You just gotta take it slow. Sometimes you gotta chisel out your next hold but you just take your time and stay quiet. If, like Dani, you've been lifting weights, running and training while in prison, it just gives you that extra level of confidence you need to get you to your destination.

She stretches her arm to the left, now grabbing hold of the railing to Carly's balcony. Upper body strength, all them pull-ups give you that. She swings monkey-bar style until both hands are holding onto the balcony. Now she pulls herself up and climbs over. "Yeeah!" she whispers, excited. She crouches down, looking across the way. No problem. No lights on. Carly has closed her curtains but she's in there. Dani can hear voices. She moves to the balcony doors, pressing her ear against the partition.

"… I'm sure there's nothing to worry about." Cazenove is anxious to get away. He's on early turn tomorrow. "But if she comes anywhere near you, call us immediately."

He smiles gently at Carly who it has to be said has gone as white as a sheet. He'd better take a quick look around, just to calm her nerves. He comes out of the living room and turns left. "May I?"

Her bedroom is the next room along. She nods mutely, waiting out in the hall as he checks. He comes out the bedroom, passes the living room and goes into the kitchen at the opposite end of the hall. On the way, he quickly pokes his head into the tiny bathroom on the left. Now he's back in the hallway, reassuring her.

"In my experience, the shock of being locked up will keep her in line. And if it doesn't, she'll be locked up until the lesson penetrates." He's already at the flat door and opens it. "Like I said, this is just a precaution. Keep this front door double locked and you should have nothing to worry about."

From where she's crouched, Dani can see the top of Cazenove's head, as he returns to his car, starts it up, reverses and drives off the estate. She watches dispassionately.

22

Soldiers

They really do look like soldiers, the way they're all standing to attention. Trevor's sat looking grim on the corner of Dani's desk in front of them.

"Listen I ain't into all the long talking and all that fucking shit. Dani got out today and she's gone missing."

The ones who didn't already know look round the room to see if this is some kind of joke or test. Trevor adds, "We have to find her soon as." He looks over to Sonny, throwing up a hand. "I don't even know where to fucking send them."

"Have you tried Charlie's?" says one.

"What about her girl?" says another.

It's hopeless. All the known places have already been checked.

Sonny shakes his head.

"Trev, we have to call Whisky."

He bows his head under the pressure.

"What if he calls the law?"

Ellis is calm.

"If he calls the law on Dani, we'll fucking do the lot of them. We know where he lives."

"Yeah but it'll be too fucking late for her, won't it?" Trevor blinks. "Anyway, how do we know?"

"How do we know what?"

He's impatient.

"Know where Whisky lives?"

Ellis points a thumb over his shoulder.

"Me and Darren dropped him home after we dropped off them ounces for Jason that time."

Sonny wheels around to face them.

"Didya?"

"Yeah, let's go lift him."

"Wait. Hold up. We have to think before we go lifting him. He's not exactly an enemy, is he?"

Trevor would prefer some action than none at all.

"Yeah, but Sonny – we ain't gonna be best buddies if Dani sends his cousin, are we?"

Sonny grunts.

"Maybe, but they bring us business and they come in with us sometimes. And," he points, "… you do business with him."

"I don't give a fuck!"

"Yeah but we gotta think about what's left tomorrow after we've torn everything up."

Trevor raises his voice above everyone's.

"I'm thinking about what Dani might be doing while we're stood here worrying about people that ain't fucking family!" He jumps up off the desk, "Fuck this! I'm gonna get Whisky. Whoever wants to come, come now and whoever wants to stay, it's on you if we don't get her back." He strides out of the room, then turns back to them, his face like thunder. "Wanna call yourself soldiers? Let's see who you really fucking are!"

In her flat, Carly has every light on. Every window is closed, the blinds are down and the curtains drawn. So where is that draught coming from? She steps out of the bathroom and into the living room opposite, where she finds that the balcony door is closed but the curtains are slightly apart. She frowns, the breath catching in her throat when she sees the splintered wood on the floor.

She spins, fearing who may be behind her, but there's no one. She grabs the phone, jabbing at the nine three times. Even if she is overpowered the call will be traced. She listens, looking frantically about her until she realises there's no dial tone. A whimper escapes from the back of her throat as she drops the phone and steps out into the hallway. It's definitely her.

She stops dead. Where are the flat keys? She'd left them in the lock after seeing the officer out. She reaches the front door in two steps, trying to open it. She's locked in.

Twelve vehicles are parked in and around the road where Whisky lives. Trevor has his game face on already as Sonny mutters, "Alright, lemme just try something Trev. If it don't work we'll all go in."

Trevor sighs. "Fucksakes!" Every second of delay could be adding another year on her sentence. "Hurry up."

Sonny takes out his phone.

There is a sound of dripping water. Carly turns. The sink is overflowing in the bathroom, because someone has turned the tap on and put the plug in. She cowers as she steps gingerly, half expecting Dani to jump at her from behind the shower curtain. She turns off the tap. The hairs on the back of her neck rise up even before she hears her. She turns back to the hallway.

"Can't trust no one, can ya?" Dani smiles a wide evil smile.

Carly sucks in air and holds her breath as Dani looks around.

"This is a small flat." She leans in close, whispering gleefully. "I bet it feels fucking smaller now you're locked in with me, don't it?"

Carly draws her head away, trying not to look directly at her. Dani steps back into the living room, smiling confidently.

"You and me, we're gonna be cell mates for a little while."

She sits down in the nearest chair, pulling the hammer from her sleeve and placing it across her lap.

"One of the reasons people like me and you don't go to the police is cos you can't fucking trust 'em."

She cracks her neck from side to side. Now she shakes her head.

"Can't trust 'em." She strokes the handle of the hammer. "Apparently there's nothing to worry about. It's just a precaution. They're gonna keep you safe." A sneer appears and disappears in an instant. "You can't trust 'em not to leave your address in a place where someone like me might find it." She smiles a small smile. "Like on the back of this."

She pulls the statement from her pocket, waving it in mid air. Carly holds herself taut though her whole body is trembling. Dani shoves the paper back in her pocket.

"They hand me your address and then they tell me not to contact you." She shrugs her shoulders "Can't trust 'em."

Now she taps her finger to her chest. "Me you can trust. I'm exactly what you think I am."

She looks up, raising her eyebrows. "I mean, obviously I'm un-fucking-stable but still you know what you're gonna get." She smiles that smile again. "Don't ya?" She throws an ankle up onto her knee. "But you know what makes me slip my fucking chain?" Her voice is getting louder. "Is someone tryna fuck about with me and my Suse."

Carly steps back as she stands suddenly, shoving the hammer down into her waistband.

"You're gonna drop them charges tomorrow."

Dani is advancing on her, pointing in her face.

"Not tomorrow night, not tomorrow afternoon, I'm talking about before the sun comes up you're gonna be sat in that cop shop telling them it's all been a horrible fucking misunderstanding."

Carly swallows.

"Cos if you don't ..." Dani is looking around. "I'm gonna come back with my people and I'm gonna burn this little shoe box down with you in it." She turns back to face the now rigid Carly. "I don't think you understand my relationship with her. Cos if you did you wouldn't try fucking about with it."

"She's scared of you." Carly gulps.

She should have kept her mouth shut. Dani looks at her with disgust.

"Fuck you talking about? She ain't scared of me!"

Carly says nothing, stepping back again as Dani leans in on her. "She is not scared of me."

"She was scared when you broke in." She tells herself to shut up!

"Who told you that?"

"Who do you think?"

Dani is frowning.

"Look, I don't know why she told you that but ..."

Carly is emboldened by the change in Dani's demeanour. "She wanted to explain why she had to leave me."

Dani's eyebrows shoot upwards.

"Why did she have to leave you then?"

"Cos you made her."

Dani has to laugh.

"How'd I do that?"

"You broke into her house, you dragged her out of the club ..."

"Oh, I dragged her now? She came because she wanted to come!"

Carly nods.

"That's just what a stalker would say."

Dani bursts out laughing.

"A what! Carly, listen to me very carefully. Susanna wants to be with me. You don't know her and you don't know what the fuck you're talking about."

Carly swallows again, jutting out her chin.

"Let her make the choice and we'll see."

Dani looks at her with something akin to pity.

"I'm starting to wonder which one of us is more sick in the head."

They stare at each other until Dani snorts, shaking her head again. She turns away, putting even more distance between them. She seems to be having a debate with herself as Carly watches her.

"I shouldn't have done that." She gestures towards Carly's hand.

Carly says nothing.

"My tailor once said to me you should ask yourself this question. If someone wrongs you, did they do it because they were weak or because they were strong?" She shrugs again. "He says the answer is always the same."

"She didn't want to go back to you."

Dani chuckles, shaking her head.

"She told me!"

"You think you know her don't you?"

Dani peers over at her. Carly's eyes are now glistening as she says, "We were planning for a baby."

Dani shakes her head in pity,

"*She* weren't."

Angry tears spring up at the corners of Carly's eyes.

Dani sighs.

"Look, I'm sorry about your hand. If you'd known about us properly you wouldn't have ended up in shit with me. I ain't letting her go so just get this fucking case sorted and I'm done warring with you, alright?" She goes to her pocket with one hand, pointing over at her with the other. "And don't let me see you in any of my Meets again."

She pulls Carly's door keys out. The statement drops out onto the floor as well.

Dani breathes through her nostrils as she bends to pick it up. Carly is holding out her hand for the keys.

"Wait a second." Dani pulls the keys back, looking down at the statement. "You better not have said any of my boys' names."

Carly blinks away tears, groaning inwardly as Dani's eyes begin to move from left to right and back again, across the paper.

"Stay where you are."

She growls this as Carly begins to edge away and darts suddenly for the kitchen, just as Dani's gaping eyes read the words "assaulted and harassed Susanna." The kitchen door slams shut with Carly on the other side of it.

I accept that I was arrested for punching and threatening Susanna Grange who is a potential witness in this case, but I would like to say that ...

The Dani that apologised not two minutes ago has blacked out. She has gone into a shock-induced stupor and the Dani that has reared up in her place is hot and howling, gnashing her teeth and flexing her jaw. The brow descends as the teeth are bared. She even looks like a different person. The rage courses through her bloodstream, burning her from inside while desperately seeking an outlet. Breathing, counting ... this Dani isn't capable of those things.

She glares up at the kitchen door. Not a sound is coming from the other side. Inside Carly is slowly, carefully opening the window above the sink. She'll climb out onto the landing and escape down the stairs. There's no lock on the kitchen door. Who ever has a lock there? That would be unsafe, wouldn't it? She eases her feet slowly from her trainers and climbs up onto the sink.

Whisky's Rover 2000 is a beautiful pillar-box red with the spare tyre on the boot. He polishes the car every week. The sound of the engine tells you it's well looked after. The problem with it is, as his dad's told him ever since he bought it, the body is too heavy for that size engine.

"You should have got the V8 3.5 litre. That would have been fast."

But Whisky is not the boy racer type. He's a businessman. He doesn't invite drama because he likes his business to run smoothly so he can get on with actually enjoying the spoils. So when he gets the text he's actually pissed off. *HELP COME NOW CARLY.*

He doesn't recognise the number it's come from, but Carly is like Tony. Telling them to stay out of trouble is like telling a baby not to put stuff in it's mouth. They're gonna do it anyway. He's called John but John just goes into a panic, asking the same fucking questions over and over instead of getting off his arse and doing something about it.

Now he's calling Simon and Abdi and rounding up people. John's a bit of a bottler to be honest. Whisky leaves him to it. He knows most people respect him. He'll probably just have to talk for Carly himself, get her out of whatever scrape she's got herself into this time. He wishes this car were faster.

Four cars back, one of Dani's soldiers drives carefully. Trevor and Sonny's car is the furthest behind.

"How we doing it?"

Sonny looks sideways at Trevor, who's not speaking. That's how he gets when he's wound up this tight.

Trevor cranes his neck to the side as Whisky's car takes a left turn up ahead.

"Cover up, pile in behind him, knock him out and get Dani the fuck out of there."

His tone suggests it was a stupid question, but Sonny says, "He's gonna know it was us ain't he? We ain't gonna be able to stop Carly telling him Dani was there. And obviously he'll work out she didn't send the text."

"So what! Can't fucking prove nothing can they?"

"You're thinking about police Trev, I'm thinking about making enemies."

Trevor looks at him incredulously.

"No one wants a fucking war with me, Son."

"Maybe not up front, but they can do things behind the scenes and claim it ain't them."

Trevor exhales loudly.

"You always wanna be the fucking diplomat, don't ya? So what you want me to do eh? Ask nicely if he wouldn't mind us going in first so we can pull Dani off his cousin?"

"She might already have been and gone Trev. If that's the case we might be talking compensation to shut them up."

"What? Are you fucking drunk! She had it coming. She's had Dani inside all that time and on top of it she's fucking giving Susanna a slap! What did she think would happen? She's lucky I never heard about it first!" He turns away angrily. "What the fuck!"

Most people would give him time to calm down now but Sonny takes a deep breath, and presses on.

"I'm thinking we stop Whisky at the door. Lift him, but like not knock him about. Then I'll explain it to him while you lot go in and get her. If she's already gone you can give Carly the standard warning and I'll persuade Whisky not to take it any further."

Trevor can't help laughing.

"Alright Son, you talk. I'll go in there and sort it."

"We don't need to hurt Whisky. He ain't done nothing wrong."

"What, apart from bringing that Carly to two fucking Meets?"

"Yeah but that's what I'm gonna show him! He was careless and that's why everything's got out of hand innit?"

"Out of hand!" Trevor laughs mirthlessly. "You reckon?"

Carly hasn't made it any further than the sink before Dani slashes at the hand holding the window frame, clamps her arm around Carly's waist and hauls her back to the kitchen floor.

Carly cries out as loud as she can, knowing the window is open.

"Shut up!"

Dani rams her fist down in her mouth.

"No! Leave me alone!"

Dani bangs her fist down again. Still Carly won't stop.

"Get off me. Help!"

Dani's eyes are blazing. "You wanna scream? OK let's scream." She grabs at the bandaged hand. Now Carly howls as she twists it this way and that.

"Stop! Please please stop!"

Downstairs Whisky is running from his car. The whole street can hear Carly. He skids as he turns into the stairwell, gasping as he is suddenly rammed up against the wall. Three men, their faces covered with scarves and hoods, hold him while others tear up the stairs at top speed.

"What did you do to her?" Dani yells. "Say it out loud!"

"No. No. Help!"

"Tell me what you did and I'll stop."

"No. You won't! Get off me!"

Dani bares her teeth, drawing the hammer from her waistband. She raises it above Carly's bandaged hand, which she has clamped down with her knee. "Yeah? You wanna put your hands on her do ya? Wanna knock her about!"

CRASH!

The front door comes off its hinges. There is banging and shouting as Dani makes the snap decision to do it anyway. They have her now. An attempt is the same sentence as doing it, ain't it? She'll make sure it's worth the punishment. She snarls as she drives her hand down hard, only to be knocked sideways by someone flying at her midriff.

Carly's sobbing and screaming alternately while Dani struggles violently with her adversary.

"Stop! Dani, stop!"

She can just about make out the words above all the shouting on the landing. She opens her eyes to see hooded men in overalls, their faces obscured. Carly has stopped making noise. Now Dani can hear what they are shouting out on the landing to the neighbours,

"Get back inside. Get back in your fucking house! What the fuck you looking at? Get back inside!"

Dani looks up at the person holding her down. Sonny's eyes look back at her. Now she hears Trevor's voice. He's scouring the flat.

"What did you come with, Dani? What tools?"

She's hyperventilating, struggling for control. She manages to point to the hammer.

"Come on! Hurry up! Where's the rest?"

She grasps at her pockets.

"Chisel," she breathes.

"What else? What else!" He's shouting in her face through the fog. She looks down at herself again.

"Blade. Stanley blade."

"I got it."

Sonny picks it up from by her knee.

"What about this?"

Someone's holding up the leather chamois. That must be Darren.

"Yeah." She nods eagerly, suddenly coming to her senses. "Yeah that's it."

"Come on." Trevor hauls her up from the floor, shoving her to the front door. "Get her out of here. Cover your face Dani."

He waits until he is the only one left inside with Carly who is still lying on the floor. They only had to tell her to be quiet once. He leans down over her, whispering into her ear, murmuring his threats and promises. When he eventually stands he tells her to get up.

"Whisky's coming. Are you hurt?"

He doesn't seem to notice her badly swollen cheek and blood coming from her nose. She shakes her head as he asks, "She didn't really get a chance to do anything, did she?"

Again she shakes her head quickly.

"Good."

He leaves.

Downstairs Sonny is speaking to Whisky while Dani sits dumbfounded in the back of the car. All around she sees cars and cars of her soldiers, their eyes smiling out at her from under hoods and behind masks, like jewels.

Treasure.

Trevor appears at the bottom of the stairs. There is a short conversation between him and Whisky, who glances quickly over at Dani before accepting Trevor's outstretched hand.

She can't take it all in.

Now Trevor goes to each car in turn.

"Get rid of those masks. Take your hoods down. Go straight home." He has an amused look on his face when he climbs in next to Sonny. "Only one didn't show."

"Who?"

Sonny frowns while Dani looks from one to the other. Trevor gives him a shake of the head.

"Let's go."

Sonny starts the engine, glancing up at Dani in the rearview mirror.

"Alright boss?"

She nods back, uncertain. Trevor looks round at her gravely.

"Don't you ever fucking pull a stunt like that again, Dani. You fucking call us and we sort it properly. You don't go off by yourself with your half assed plans."

She lowers her eyes as he continues, "Look behind you. You see how many fucking boys have put themselves on the line for you tonight?"

She glances up.

"Who didn't show?"

He gives her a look of warning before turning away to face the front.

"Drop me home, Sonny."

She remains silent until they arrive at Trevor's house. He opens the car door without looking back.

"Thanks Trev."

"Fuck off!"

She smiles to herself as Trevor closes his front door. Now she looks back up at Sonny.

"So who was the one then? Who didn't show?"

He shakes his head.

"Ain't you got somewhere to be?"

She smiles.

Epilogue

t's almost midnight when they arrive.

"Give us your phone. I don't wanna frighten her."

It rings only twice.

"It's me, Suse."

"Are you OK?"

"Yeah, yeah. Look, I'm sorry it's so late."

"It's OK. I was worried. What's happened? Have you been fighting?"

Dani is laughing.

"You sound different. What's going on?"

"Has Sonny been round?"

"Today? No."

"He's gonna knock on your door in a minute. Let him in, alright."

She sits up in the bed.

"Why?"

"Cos I've got something for you."

Dani steps into the lift, her knees almost buckling with the excitement. The signal is breaking up.

"Dani?"

There's a knock at the door.

Printed in Great
Britain
by Amazon

32339918R00168